Field of Flowers

KAYLEE DAVENPORT

ISBN 979-8-89309-786-3 (Paperback)
ISBN 979-8-89309-787-0 (Digital)

Copyright © 2024 Kaylee Davenport
All rights reserved
First Edition

All rights reserved. No part of this publication may be reproduced, distributed, or transmitted in any form or by any means, including photocopying, recording, or other electronic or mechanical methods without the prior written permission of the publisher. For permission requests, solicit the publisher via the address below.

Covenant Books
11661 Hwy 707
Murrells Inlet, SC 29576
www.covenantbooks.com

*To everyone who believed I could do it,
And to everyone who helped me along the way*

*To be shrouded in darkness is not a choice;
the choice is whether to go towards the people with flashlights
or to turn your back and walk away.*

The End to a Story

This story starts at the end, with the funeral of a girl I once knew. I could imagine all the people there to see her one last time. In reality, she was a very popular girl, though there was one person who didn't show up. That person was me. Now that may sound absurd to many, considering the fact that she was my best friend. It was for a reason that at the time I thought was reasonable.

In truth, *I killed her*. I killed Daisy Harrow. So while people cried over her casket, I sat alone in my room. Next to me was a photo album that I never got to fill. If someone saw me at that very moment, they would call me pathetic.

Now, don't turn away, now knowing how the story ends, dear reader. For every story has a beginning, even if the beginning is truly the end.

For you to understand, we must start at the very beginning, the true start of this story...

Humble Beginnings

Nearly thirty-five years ago, a woman from Chicago had decided to study abroad. She shuffled through many colleges and countries. In the end, however, she decided to go with her first choice, France.

Her family called her crazy as she packed up her whole life into a few boxes. She arrived in a new country knowing virtually nothing. All she knew was her love for dance and art. She had no friends in what seemed like a new world for her.

The woman would often study at a local café down nearly a block from her dormitory. At that café was a guy who carefully studied the arts of coffee and pastries. He hoped that one day he could open a café of his own. His nervous hands would spark up a conversation after spilling coffee on the woman. They would exchange names and numbers. Marissa to Elliot and Elliot to Marissa.

In a turn of events, the two would start dating. From there Marissa would choose to move to a town right outside of Paris with Elliot. This would be against her parents' wishes, of course.

If neighbors were to comment on the two, they would say "Simply meant to be!" That statement couldn't be any truer.

One night, after having a picnic by the Eiffel tower, Elliot proposed. From there they would have two children, a boy, Louis, and a girl, Eden—me.

However, after having me, my mother would grow sick. After years of enduring this sickness, she would grow frailer. When I turned seven, we would be forced to move to America. My mother's family from Chicago would welcome us with open arms. Here my father opened the café of his dreams. One filled with books and the best pastries.

Mother would eventually get better and beat her illness. In the end, we would ultimately decide to stay in Chicago.

As I got older, I helped out more with the café. I would usually be on the floor stocking books or cleaning up. Just all the menial tasks. However, working such tasks lead me to the beginning you've been waiting for—the day I met Daisy Harrow.

1

A Summer to Remember

It all started on a hot day in the middle of a blazing summer, before junior year. I looked up from stocking the shelves and took a look around. There were tons of people in the store that day; it was fairly unusual. In some ways, it made me angry. A social media influencer posted about it for the whole "Support the small businesses" movement. Then as if it was magic, tons of people began showing up. Not to support us, but because a "celebrity" had been here.

My father acted like he won the lottery or struck gold. He would walk around with a cheesy smile, greeting the customers. He even began marketing pastries as "her favorite."

I turned back and pulled my book cart to the next aisle and put books in their proper places. *Fantasy to fantasy, romance to romance.* I heard the door chime from across the store as I turned back to my cart. I, without looking over, gave the usual greeting. "Welcome to Aubert Books!" I didn't pay any attention to it and just continued to stock the shelves.

A group of girls had walked through the door. They laughed as they pointed their phones in each other's faces. Something about their laughs seemed oddly familiar. I took my focus off the books for a quick moment and peeked out of the aisle. At first glimpse, I felt my knees get weaker. The group of girls went to my school.

Now you may be saying, "Hey, Eden, it's just a few girls from your school. No big deal!" Now that wouldn't be the issue if it was anyone else. Yet this group and I weren't exactly on good terms.

During freshman year, I slipped in the cafeteria walking to my table. Long story short, my soup flew and ruined Rose's uniform. They had never forgiven me, nor had I been back to the cafeteria since.

Out of pure instinct, I decided to make a break for the back room. Now, that would've worked, but nothing ever goes my way. My apron, which was uniform policy, had gotten caught on the book cart. And along with me and my dignity, the cart came toppling down.

I sat stupidly on the floor in a pile of books. I took a frustrated breath in and hoped nobody saw.

"Oh! Are you okay, miss? Let me help you."

Great, just great. "I don't need help. I work here," I said as I lifted the cart and stacked books back on. The girl next to me started grabbing books as well. "Let me help, please!" It seemed so sincere that I looked up.

We stared at each other blankly for what seemed like ages. Kneeling in front of me was the one and only Daisy Harrow.

"Wait, you're Eden Aub—" I covered her mouth so the others wouldn't hear.

Daisy was the oddball of her friend group. She was kind and sweet, while her friend group was cold and nasty. Daisy was even known as the goddess of Lincoln Academy, and she looked like it too. She was your typical beauty with long blonde hair and green eyes. This was as opposed to my short dark hair and deep dark eyes.

Daisy pulled my hand off her mouth. "Don't worry, I won't let anyone know that you're here, especially not my friends."

I felt a comforting sense of relief wash over me. I held my pinky up, "Promise?"

Daisy had a genuine warm smile as she latched her pinky with mine. "I promise!"

I stood up and brushed off my knees. "Daisy! Where did you go?" a girl called out.

Daisy gave me an apologetic look. "I gotta go." I gave a half wave as she walked off and joined her group again.

I peeked around the corner as the girls sat down at the café counter. I then carefully tiptoed to the back room.

I slumped down on the couch as my dad walked over. "Girl, why are you not working?" I looked up at him and gave an unsure smile. "Go mop the back," he said with a stern look. I sighed and got back up. It wasn't long before Daisy and her friend group left the café that day. However, that wouldn't be the last time I see Daisy Harrow.

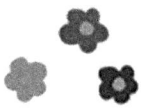

A few days went by, and everything went normally in the shop. We got our usual customers like students, workers, and even those who enjoy coffee with a good book.

On this particular day, I was in charge of the café, in place of my brother. I was starting to forget about a few days ago, as if it had never happened. Then as if by fate, the bell chimed. "Hello, welcome to—" I stopped midsentence and ducked behind the counter.

Walking around the store was Daisy. I was completely sure that she wouldn't come back. The customers gave me weird looks as I sat on the floor. I do admit that I overreacted just a bit.

Daisy slowly approached the counter and sat down. "I knew I would find you here."

I propped myself up with a look of defeat plastered across my face. I gave a forced smile. "What can I get you?"

Daisy gave me a sideways smile in return. "Aw c'mon, you can be a bit more enthusiastic about this."

I relaxed my face and leaned my arms on the counter in front of her. "Fine." I gently laughed. "What can I get for you?"

Daisy leaned back as if she had to think for a moment. "Could I maybe get a fruit tart?" I paused for a moment. She chose the one thing that was baked by me.

I'd been slowly receiving training in the café from my brother and father. They'd taught me to brew coffee, make specialty drinks, and bake some pastries.

"Are you sure?" I asked because, of course, I had no confidence in it. This was the first time my pastries had been put out for sale.

"I'm sure!" she said with a smile to me. I hesitantly turned around like a gear crying for oil. I grabbed the fruit tart and placed it in front of her. I admit, visually it was pretty good.

Daisy took a bite, and I winced. However, instead of being greeted by a foul remark, she was silent. Her face gave off such an expression that it could need a whole new name. Like an expression of impressiveness and shock. Daisy turned her head toward me and smiled, "Eden, this is hands down the best fruit tart I have ever had!"

It caught me by surprise. "Really!"

Daisy nodded her head before looking around. "Could you possibly point me toward the fantasy section?"

I lifted my hand toward the corner of the shop, and she scurried off to find it. Daisy had yet again caught me by surprise. Most teenagers stop by not to buy books but for our café section.

She returned with a book in her hands. It had an orange cover with a Ferris wheel of flowers on the front. I knew exactly what book it was. Daisy sat back down on the barstool. "I was looking for this book. I saw it on your cart the other day. But taking it would be rude."

I stared at her blankly. "You read *Carnival of Flowers*?" I had never once met someone else who does, until now.

"Wait, you know about *Carnival of Flowers*?" she asked me.

"Um, it's only my favorite series ever!"

Her eyes lit up like fire on a cold night. Daisy leaned forward and grabbed my hand with both of hers. With a smile, she asked, "What time does your shift end?"

I looked down at my watch and then back to her. "Um, in about two hours?"

She reached into her purse and pulled out her credit card. "Then I'll wait."

After paying for her items, she hopped off the barstool and sat down on the couches. I didn't think she would stay for the whole two hours, but she did. I peeked up at her every so often as I continued serving customers. She just sat there reading her book with a huge smile across her face. I admit that I even caught myself smiling, though I quickly wiped it off my face.

Eventually, my brother walked into the shop. He walked up to me and leaned on the counter. His hair, which he promised he'd cut, was still as scruffy as ever. "I told you E'ed that you'd be good at this!"

I gave him a petty look as I reached up and grabbed his hair. "And I told you to cut your hair!"

I released his mop of a head and began untying my apron. I leaned into the back room where my dad sat on the couch, watching his cooking shows. It was funny how he got mad at me for sitting down when he did this.

"Louis is here! I'm clocking out" He looked over at me and shooed his hand. I shut the door and crumpled a piece of paper before throwing it at Louis.

"What's this?"

I turned around as I switched my shoes. "A supply list for you to order."

He gave me a look of frustration, "Why does it always have to be me? I just got here!" I ignored him and walked out from behind the counter. Surprisingly Daisy was already standing there waiting.

She stood against the wall with her book in her arm. It was at this moment that I realized her outfit. She wore a tucked-in white shirt that had outlines of flowers and their names below them. The shirt was tucked into loose blue denim shorts that were secured with a brown belt. She must've noticed me looking because she kicked her right foot up. "These shoes are my favorite!" They were white gym shoes with a blue logo and tan accents.

"They're really cool!"

Daisy gave a big grin. "You bet they are!" She then looked at her book and back at me. "Do you think we can discuss *Carnival of Flowers*?

I excitedly nodded my head. "Does my house work?" She nodded back, and we began walking.

I do admit I was a bit nervous and in over my head. I had never invited anyone over to my house before. We began walking down the busy sidewalks of downtown toward my house.

Daisy stopped and looked up at the passing clouds. "You know, there is one place I really want to visit."

I looked at her while glancing at the frustrated people passing us. "And where would that be?" I asked. "In *Carnival of Flowers*, they talk about this field of flowers that was so breathtaking just to look at it! A field filled with tons of different types of flowers."

She looked back at me. "That's where I want to go. I want to go to the field of flowers!" I smiled at her. It was the same place I wanted to go see. "We can see it together, one day," I said as I held my pinky up.

She latched hers with mine once more and said, "It's a promise!"

We arrived at the train station a few blocks later. I didn't live close to the café but I didn't live far at the same time. It was maybe a fifteen-minute train ride. My house was in one of the suburbs not too far off the city.

"Wait, so this means you ride the train to school every day?" Daisy said as we waited on the platform. I nodded as I sat down on a nearby bench. Daisy followed and sat down next to me. It felt kind of weird. Daisy was going home with me. What if I was a murderer or rather she was?

Yet at the same time, she didn't feel like a stranger at all. She felt like a friend whom I'd had for a long time even though we had just met.

Daisy leaped off the bench and sprinted down the platform, pointing ahead. "The train is coming!"

I got up and walked next to her. "Have you never been on a train before?"

She looked down at her shoes and laughed with a calm smile, "I have." She looked up at me and gave a smile that felt like hitting a wall. "But that was a long time ago!" The train screeched into the station as I gave her a blank expression. I caught myself as the train came to a complete stop. "Let's get on," I said.

Daisy hopped onto the train and tugged at my shirt. "Can we sit up top?"

I began laughing at her look of determination. "Sure, let's go."

I had given her the window seat so she could look at the passing scenery. And just as I had imagined, she did exactly what I thought. Daisy peered out the window with an amazed look on her face.

I sat back in my seat with a smile. It was as if her smile was contagious. I grabbed my earphones out of my pocket and placed them in my ears. I had always found the noises on the train to be a bit headache-inducing. I sunk into the seat and tried to think of what I was gonna do when we got to my house.

However, I was so caught up in my thoughts that I didn't even see her. Daisy had pulled the left earbud out of my ear and placed it in hers. I gave her a surprised look as I jolted my head toward her. She leaned closer to me, and I felt my face getting hot as her blonde hair brushed against it.

"Is this the new song from Monkeys?"

I nodded my head as she backed into her seat again.

"I like them. In some ways, their music is calming," Daisy said as she looked at me.

I smiled at her. "They're a really cool band."

We laughed and began talking about our favorite music artist. It came as a surprise to me, we had fairly similar music tastes. Of course, they had their differences here and there. But it really showed me that two people may seem different; however, they may not be as different as they look.

The speakers chimed and announced the next station. "This is our stop," I said, reaching out for her hand as I stood up. She began getting up as the train started slowing down until it came to a hard stop.

Now, to someone who rides the train almost every day, I could easily stand perfectly fine. But to someone who isn't quite experienced, it's not going to end so well. I realized this and turned back around to see Daisy beginning to fall. I grabbed her hand with one of mine and my other hand on the rail. I swooped her close to me and propped her back on her feet. Daisy gave me a blank expression.

"Be careful!" I said as she took a deep breath and collected herself. We headed down the narrow staircase of the train car, then out the doors.

"Oh wow! This area is so pretty!" Daisy gasped.

My neighborhood did have its own kind of feel to it. It was kinda dark and cozy. Large trees lined the sidewalks and blocked out most of the light. I liked it that way.

We rounded the corner to see my house. It wasn't much to show off, though I loved my house. It reminded me of a cottage in the forest, given all the tall trees. It was one of the older houses in my neighborhood since, well, most of the others had been knocked down and rebuilt.

Daisy looked at me as I opened the gate. "Your house is so adorable!" she said as she looked around and gawked at it. I walked up to my door, which at the time was a deep blue kinda color. I turned the key in the handle and opened it. My house had just finished being remodeled, so it looked pretty nice.

"Feel free to take off your shoes and leave them by the door," I said as I grabbed a bowl in the kitchen. I turned around to see that she had already taken off her shoes. "Oh, sorry," she said, laughing. I continued to pour a variety of chips into the bowl in front of me. "It's sorta instinctive." Daisy laughed.

"It's no big deal. Make yourself at home." I only said that because that's what they say in movies and TV shows. In reality, I had no idea what the hell I was supposed to do.

"Let's hang out in my room," I said to her as I began to head toward the staircase. The way my house was set up was interesting. When you first walk in the front door, to the left of you would be the living room, and to your right would be the kitchen. Straight ahead you were greeted by the dining room and a hidden staircase to your right.

"A hidden staircase! Your house just keeps getting cooler!" Daisy said as she brushed her hand against the wall as we ascended the stairs.

I reached for my door handle and opened up my familiar wooden door. My room wasn't anything too special. It was your standard four-wall room polluted with band posters, records, and plants. They say rooms can tell a lot about a person. All mine said was that I cared a bit too much about music.

Daisy took a look at all my walls one by one, then she stopped at my shelf of vinyl records. She gently brushed her hand across each one until she got to one in particular. It was a blue cover with a young child swimming toward a dollar. "You like *Nirvana*?" I asked. She released the vinyl from her fingertips and turned to look at me.

"It was my dad's favorite band…"

I reached up and pulled it off the shelf. "We could listen to it if you want?" Daisy gave me another smile. Gosh, she smiles a lot. I don't mind, though.

I opened up a sage-green case that was on my dresser. I revealed it to be a record player. I had just gotten it a Christmas prior, so I was stoked to use it whenever I could.

I placed the vinyl on and lowered the needle onto the record's ridges. The silence was followed by the familiar guitar, which was then followed by the roaring drums. This song was the first in the album *Nevermind*. It was easily my favorite and competitively the best song from the band. Daisy seemed to like it as well, maybe even more than I did. She seemed to know all the lyrics. Within seconds, we found ourselves jumping around and singing along. To think the frilly goddess of Lincoln Academy would be into this kind of music.

The time seemed to pass me by, and before I knew it, the sun had already gone down. We had just talked and talked. It was as if we never could run out of something to talk about. We talked like old friends catching up. About books, music, shows, and movies; anything really.

I peered down at my phone and caught a glimpse of the time. "Oh, it's getting late. Your parents are gonna be worried about you!" I hobbled around my room trying to get my socks on.

"Don't worry, nobody's gonna worry about me."

I paused for a moment and looked back at her. "Why?"

Her viridescent eyes seemed to turn cold. "My mom is away on business in New York, and my stepdad is never home."

I sat down on the floor next to her. "Wait, so you've been home alone?"

Daisy smiled and began laughing. "I'm fine, really!"

I didn't believe it. Not for a second. "Do you wanna stay for dinner?" It was as if I said the magic words to her. Yet she still seemed hesitant.

I grabbed her hands in mine. "I'll make sure you get on before the last train!"

Daisy began laughing again. "Well, if you insist. I guess I'll have to stay!" She then grinned at my excited expression. "I mean, just look at you."

I covered my face as I laughed. "Hush!"

My father knocked on my door and peeked in. It was as if I had planned it. "Is your friend staying for dinner?" I nodded toward him. "Well, c'mon! It's ready." He grinned and seemingly skipped down the hall. It was screaming out "Eden finally has a friend over!" It annoyed me, though I couldn't argue with it either. I'd never really had friends.

I stood up and offered my hand to Daisy. "Let's go eat." She gave a big grin and hopped up. We slid down the hallway with our socks like children. I found it hard to believe that we were gonna be juniors this year. I almost fell down the stairs like an idiot. Thankfully, I caught myself.

When we reached the bottom of the staircase, my father ushered us over to the dining room. This caught me by surprise. Usually, we eat on the island in the kitchen, or in our rooms, for that matter.

The dining room table was set nicely; this was quite a rare sight. My mother finished placing down the last plates and turned toward us. "And who is this lovely young lady?"

Daisy smiled and gave a small wave. "My name is Daisy Harrow. I go to school with Eden."

My mother gave us a warm smile and gestured for us to sit down. "It's nice to meet you, sweetheart."

Daisy and I sat down across from each other as my father brought in steaming plates of food. He had cooked one of my favorites, beef bourguignon. In short, it's like a red wine–based beef stew. That's based on my knowledge of it. To top it all, my father brought over a basket of freshly baked rolls. Daisy was practically drooling at this point. I gently nudged her foot under the table and grinned. She looked up at me and said, "What? I like bread." We all erupted in laughter at her comment.

Dinner was delicious and ended pretty quickly. I put on my shoes, and Daisy did the same.

"We're off!" I shouted as we left out the door. Even though it was night, it was still blaring hot out. The street lights were on, and Daisy and I walked side by side down the sidewalk. "You know, I had a lot of fun tonight."

I turned and smiled at her. "Me too. I haven't laughed like that in a while."

She then frantically reached into her pocket and pulled out her phone. "It completely slipped my mind! Let's exchange numbers!" I pulled out my phone as well. We exchanged phones and put in our contact info. "There! Now we're official friends!" She handed my phone back to me with a cheesy grin.

I looked at her contact profile to see that she put herself as "Daisy" with a heart next to it. I began laughing. "Why the heart?"

She tried to argue through her laughter. "It's cute! Unlike your basic one!"

I crossed my arms. "It's so cheesy!"

Daisy looked up at me. "So?"

I tried to hold it in, but I couldn't stop laughing until we got to the train station.

When we got there, the train was just pulling up, and it came to a screeching halt. The doors opened, and Daisy faced me. She hugged me. It felt warm and comforting, even on this humid night.

To me, she whispered, "Be sure to text me, okay, Eden?" Her arms unlatched softly from my waist. Daisy was much shorter than I was. Like a tree and a squirrel. I find that analogy funny. She stepped onto the train and watched me from the doorway. "I'll text you when I get home!"

"Don't fall again when the train stops!" I shouted. She began laughing as the doors shut. I stood on the platform and watched the train pull away until I could no longer see it.

I turned back and started heading home. I put my hand over my face. I felt like a completely different person but in a good way. Like old wounds finally starting to heal. I had a friend. But not just any friend, it was Daisy Harrow.

I arrived back home and entered through the front door again. I was slipping off my shoes when I noticed my mother sitting in the living room. She was sitting in her armchair next to the lamp.

"Promise that you'll take care of that girl," she said.

I walked closer to her. "Huh?"

My mother stood up and passed me. "She brings out a part of you that you locked away years ago."

I didn't understand what she meant at the time. I just brushed it off like everything else. That day was just the beginning of our summer together.

II

To See Bursting Colors

Daisy had stopped by the shop almost every day since then. I began wondering how she was even getting here. She would show up at random times; no day was the same. Nine in the morning one day, three in the afternoon the next.

After my shift, Daisy and I would head over to my house. I found out that we both love playing video games. I hate to admit it, but she was way better than me at it. This had been going on for two weeks already. You would think my father would be annoyed at this point, but I think he's cheering me on.

However, today was different in the cafe; Daisy never showed up. I thought to myself, "Maybe she finally got tired of me?" The café was closing early today because it was the Fourth of July. We only opened for a few hours; I don't know why we opened in the first place.

I checked the door as the day went on. Nine in the morning: no Daisy; eleven in the morning: no Daisy; Closing: still no Daisy. I felt kind of stupid for being so eager. Like I expected her to show. It's not like she said she was coming today. I just sucked it up and began closing.

I was wiping down the café counters and cleaning the machines. Louis should've done this before he left. If only he cared about his job as much as he cared about flirting with the female customers. Then again, I also had to give him some credit. We probably wouldn't have half our regulars if it weren't for him.

I crouched down to organize the coffee when I heard the door chime. "Sorry, we're closed!" I shouted out and continued sorting. But the person didn't leave. Instead, they started walking closer.

"Could you make an exception for me?"

Daisy? I stood up quickly, bashing my head on the counter as I stood up.

"Oh my gosh! Eden, be careful!"

Daisy stood in front of me wearing a concerned look on her face. She reached out and gently rubbed where I hit my head. "I was almost thinking you weren't going to show."

Daisy began laughing. "So you missed me?"

I just stood silently. I didn't want to admit it. "You wish!" I said, grinning as I took her hand off my head.

"You're so mean!"

Daisy sat down on her usual barstool and kicked her legs. I reached into the pastry case and pulled out the last fruit tart before placing it in front of her. "Am I really that mean?"

Daisy gave a sideways grin before digging a fork into the tart. She ate silently, but I would catch her smiling occasionally.

I slammed my hands on the counter. "Okay! What's up?"

She looked up at me with an eager smile before putting her finger over her lips. "I have a surprise for you." She put the fork down. "So c'mon and finish up!" I was kinda confused, but I trusted her word and finished up.

I put my apron on its dedicated hook and kicked off my work shoes. Daisy stood near the entrance of the shop with her hands behind her back. I looked up at her as I tied my shoes, "So what's this so-called surprise?"

Daisy looked up and hummed as if she had to think. "No hints! Just trust me."

Daisy led me out of the store and to the parking lot out back. The only car left in the lot was a beautiful 1969 *Mustang* convertible. It was so beautifully preserved that it was almost brand-new. "Ya like it? I just got it out of the shop today."

I looked at her all excited. "This is amazing! This car costs a fortune—"

Then it hit me. I had completely forgotten that Daisy was way more well-off than I was.

"It was my dad's," she said, smiling.

I brushed my hand on the leather seats. "Did he gift it to you?"

Daisy looked over at me. "I guess you can say that."

Daisy pulled out a light-purple bandanna from her pocket and tied it over her hair. I stood confused. "What are you waiting for? Let's go!" she said, grinning at me. I smiled and walked over to the passenger side door. I brushed my hand on the shiny metal handle and pulled the door open. This was one of my dreams right here, sitting right in front of me. I gingerly sat down on the leather seat.

Daisy spun a key ring around on her finger grinning. "Just wait until you hear this baby start!" I was waiting, almost impatiently. She twisted the key into the ignition, and the car started up.

"It's so smooth!" I screamed. I was all giddy over a classic car. Like I couldn't contain my happiness. She reached up and adjusted the mirror before we set off.

We blasted music and sang the lyrics slightly off as the wind blew our hair. I still had no idea where she was taking me. I didn't focus on it and just enjoyed the ride. We headed downtown, and I just admired all the buildings around us. Even though I see them nearly every day they still seem so breathtaking to me.

We then drove under the big Chinatown gate. I looked around at all the beautiful buildings. "Is this *the* surprise?" I asked.

Daisy looked at me. "Hmm, it's part of it but not the big surprise!" We pulled into a nearby pay-to-park and hopped out. Daisy smiled. "Ah! I just love coming here!"

I shut the car door behind me. "I don't know if I've ever been here."

She paused and looked at me as if I killed a part of her. "What!" Daisy grabbed my hand. "That's it! I'm giving you the whole food experience!" We ran down the crowded sidewalks, smiling and laughing all the way. I swear people were looking at us like we were crazy. We ran until we almost reached the end of the main strip.

There stood a very low-key restaurant. Upon entering, we were greeted by a beautiful koi pond display and a grand wooden staircase that led to a second level. I would've never guessed that this beautiful restaurant was here.

Daisy raced up the stairs. "I have a reservation. Let's go!" I followed her up the large stairs. I couldn't help but look at the beautiful lighting above me. When I reached upstairs, I saw the restaurant scattered with clothed tables. The walls were filled with beautiful murals and woodworking. The waitress seated us at a table next to the huge window in the very corner. It overlooked the rest of the Chinatown strip and all of its beauty.

Daisy sat down on the chair next to me and handed a menu over. "I'm gonna order dim sum," she said before intensely gazing at the menu.

"Dim sum?" I questioned.

The menu slid out of her hands. "You don't know what it is?" She glared. I shook my head no. She let out a big sigh in response. "Have you ever lived before? It's basically like buns and dumplings, but they are all steamed in little wooden baskets." Daisy stopped and thought for a second. "Here! I'm gonna order some of my favorites for you to try."

I nodded. "Okay, uh, let's give this a try."

We checked delicious-sounding items off on a menu sheet, and the waitress came and collected it. I tried to get her to give me hints about this *surprise*, but she wasn't budging. I eventually gave up and decided to let it play out.

Daisy was talking about how she finished the new book in the *Carnival of Flowers* series already.

"Did you know that the beginning of the book series takes place in Chicago?"

I jolted my head over. "Wait, even I didn't know that one!"

She gave a big smile. "The author just recently made a statement about it. That statement was among another announcement…"

I looked over at her. "What announcement?"

She slumped down. "There is only one book left until the series comes to a close."

It was crazy hearing that, though I kinda expected it. *Carnival of Flowers* had been going on for six years at this point.

"I'm kinda happy it's ending." She continued, "We finally get to see how it ends."

I admit that I was a bit happy too. "Same for me, though it's sad."

Daisy nodded. "It's always gonna be sad saying goodbye to something you devoted so much time to." She was completely right.

The waiter came over pushing a cart. "For you. Be careful, it's hot," he said as he placed the wooden baskets on the table one by one. Daisy seemed ecstatic watching them get placed down.

"Okay, try this one first. It's a pork bun!" She placed a soft white bun on my plate before placing one on hers. "This one is by far my favorite." She giddily smiled. I picked up the pork bun and blew on it before taking a bite. Though I burnt my tongue, they were delicious.

"Holy crap! This is amazing!"

Daisy just gave me a smirk. "Yeah, and I can't believe that you've never had it before." I tried a whole bunch more delicious steamed foods, including a custard-filled bun made to look like little pigs.

Daisy and I eventually left the restaurant feeling so very full. We began walking down the street toward the car.

"Hold up! Let's stop here," I said. I took a look around and found out that we were in front of a small boba café. The café was filled with beautiful fake plants, paper umbrellas, and had a sweet sorta smell to it.

"So what are you gonna get?"

I looked at the menu and then at her. "I don't know. I've never had boba before."

Daisy gripped my shoulders. "You're killing me here, Eden!" She glared at the menu for a minute before crossing her arms.

"Do you like sweet stuff?"

"No, I'm not a big fan."
"Any allergies?"
"No."
"Then I got the perfect drink."

I took a deep breath and sat down on a seat. Daisy glared down at her watch as if she was waiting for something to happen. "Order for Harrow!" A lady called out as she placed two drinks on the counter. Daisy rushed over and handed me mine. I was shocked to see that the drink was bright purple.

"What is this?" I asked her concernedly.

Daisy gave a small grin. "It's purple yam, of course! Just take a sip."

I was extremely scared to take a sip, but for her, I sucked it up and took a swig. It was shockingly good. The drink wasn't too sweet but not bitter at the same time. At the bottom were chewy, brown tapioca pearls that accented the drink perfectly. I had caught myself judging the drink like the café worker I am.

I looked back up at Daisy. "It's really good!"

She gave a big smile. "Just leave it to the foodie!" Daisy took a sip of her drink. It was brown and gave off a very sweet smell.

"What did you get?" I asked her.

She lifted her drink. "It's a brown sugar oolong milk tea!" It was quite a mouthful of a name. She placed the drink into my hands. "Here, try it. It's my favorite."

I took a small sip, and I admit it was not my style of drink. It was sweet, and you could taste the brown sugar. "Not my kind of drink, to be honest."

She sighed. "I figured, but it was worth a shot."

We grabbed some napkins and headed out of the café.

"Are you sure you don't want me to pay you back for all of this?" I asked.

She smiled at me. "Nope! It's all my treat." Even though she said that, I still felt bad. "Wait, let's stop here for a second!"

Daisy ran ahead to a small flower shop. She squatted down and smelled the beautiful flowers.

"Flowers are one of my favorite things."

I bent down next to her. "And why is that?"

She picked up a blue flower and held it in her hands. "Humans are a lot like flowers. We spend time growing and maturing, then we open to show others our beauty. Some flowers choose not to open up, and that's okay. And once we serve our purpose, we pass along to make way for new life and opportunities for other flowers."

I brushed my hand along a flower's petals. "Like flowers, we're all delicate but so beautiful."

Daisy looked at me. "See, you get it. Some flowers just last longer than others." She peered down at her watch. "Let's get going!" Daisy grabbed my hand, and we ran back to her car.

We drove down the city toward Millennium Park; in the distance, I could see the lake. The sun was particularly bright today as it began to slowly lower above the water.

Daisy pulled into a parking spot. "We're here." I looked up to see a Ferris wheel standing high on a pier above the stagnant water.

"Are we at Navy Pier?" I asked.

Daisy looked at me, "Surprise! But that's only part of it."

We hopped out of the car and began walking toward the pier. Daisy glared up at the sky. "The sun should fully set soon, huh?" I nodded my head as we began walking onto the pier.

There were carnival games, rides, and food stalls lined up all down the walkway. I began thinking back, *I don't think I've ever really been out here like this. Maybe once or twice for a field trip.*

Daisy and I raced over to the carnival rides and began trying to ride them all. We got on this one spinner ride, and I got so sick that I threw up.

I was slumped down on a bench as Daisy returned with a bottle of water.

"Never again!" I grumbled.

Daisy fanned me with a magazine as she tried to hold back her laughter. She looked down at her watch once again and back at me. "What if we ride the Ferris wheel for our last ride?"

I sat up. "I think I'll be able to tolerate it." She smiled at me, and I stood up with her and reached out. "Let's go!"

We walked over to the Ferris wheel to be greeted by a long line. Daisy seemed worried at this point. Every minute we spent in line, she grew more anxious, frequently checking her watch over and over. We slowly, but steadily, progressed forward in the line. In about thirty minutes or so, we reached the front. Daisy finally calmed down when we sat down on the cart.

"Why do you keep checking your watch?" I asked.

Daisy paused for a moment. "You'll see." Before we knew it, we were at the highest point of the Ferris wheel. The rotation came to a halt, and we stood in place. Daisy checked her watch before quickly looking back up.

"Look over there!" she said, pointing her finger out into the distance toward the lake. With a loud screeching noise, a light flew up into the sky where it popped into a million colors—fireworks. I soon understood what the surprise was. It was the sweetest thing a friend had ever done for me. "Happy Fourth of July, Eden."

I turned to her. "To you too."

The sky was filled with bursting colors. I almost couldn't keep my eyes off them. But for a second, I turned to Daisy; her face was prettier than the fireworks at that moment.

She looked at me with an expression full of astonishment. "Aren't they beautiful?" Indeed, they were beautiful.

She reached into her tote bag, which was next to her on the seat, and pulled out a purple instant camera. "Let's take a photo together." She scooted to the seat next to me and leaned up on my shoulder. "Smile!" she said before the camera clicked.

I began laughing. "Don't we have cameras on our phones?" I asked.

Daisy laid her head on my chest and shook the photo. "Well, we could, but I like to think that these last longer."

She stayed lying on me, and we watched as the last fireworks shot into the sky. It made me think again how just a few weeks ago I didn't know Daisy. Now, she felt like someone I'd known for years.

The Ferris wheel began to spin again, and Daisy sat up. I almost didn't want it to move.

"Let's try some of the food and games that they have when we get back down!" she said, sparkling.

I covered my smiling face. "Sure, whatever you want."

When the cart reached the bottom, the employee unlocked the door, and we hopped out. "Race ya!" Daisy said before taking off toward the stalls. I laughed as I tried to catch up with her. Even though she was short, she was fast. She easily beat me and grinned when I caught up to her. "For someone who has long legs, you're slow!" She laughed.

I rested my hand on her head as I caught my breath, "So what first?"

Daisy took a look around. "Corn dogs, then the balloon popper!"

She grabbed my hand, and we ran to the corn dog stand together. I got a regular one while hers had cheese in it. We then raced over to the balloon popper game. I held both corn dogs in my hands as she strategically threw darts toward the board of balloons. I don't think I've ever seen anyone look so cool. We played tons of games like the water guns and bottle stand, half of which were rigged.

By the end of the night, Daisy had been complaining that her feet were hurting. I soon found myself walking down the pier with her on my back. I thought of it as repaying her for today.

"I noticed that you have an accent. Where are you from?"

I winced. She had noticed the one thing I wished nobody would've. The very thing I worked so hard to hide. I reluctantly replied, "France." I was awaiting the same harassment I had been met with years ago.

"What! That's so cool!" she said, gripping my shoulders.

I was taken aback. "It's cool?"

She leaned her head on my shoulder. "It's so cool being from somewhere else! Makes me wish that I was sometimes. What made you think it's not cool?"

I took a deep breath and sighed. "I moved here when I was seven, and my original tongue is French, so I had to learn English and catch up. I had joined school in fifth grade and had a pretty heavy accent."

Daisy snickered. "That sounds so cute!"

I looked at the ground. "But the other kids didn't think so."

She gave a sympathetic "*oh*" and got quiet for a second.

"Don't feel sorry for me. It's all in the past!" I tried to laugh it off, but it wasn't all in the past. It was the reason why I was so scared of friends or anyone getting too close for a long time. Sometimes I still had nightmares of the laughing and mocking.

"It still affects you, doesn't it?"

She was right. "I'm fine, really!"

She gave a suspicious "*okay*" and let the topic go.

We began walking down the sidewalk toward the car at this point. I could feel people staring.

"Can I touch your hair?"

It was a weird question. "Why do you want to?"

Daisy began laughing. "Well, because it's so short and fluffy. It looks so soft!"

I began laughing with her. "Fine, go ahead." I felt like a dog as she gently brushed her fingers through my hair.

"What shampoo do you use? It's so soft!"

I began laughing again. "Whatever my dad buys."

"Well, he knows what he's doing."

We reached the car, and I placed Daisy back onto her feet. She stood and gazed in the direction of the lake. "School is gonna start soon. We only have a few weeks left."

I didn't wanna think about it. I wanted to stay in this summer forever. Yet time waits for none.

I sat down in the passenger seat, and Daisy twisted the key into the ignition. It was time to head home. She went the extra mile and drove me straight home; she could've just left me at the train station.

We pulled up in front of my house faster than I expected, and I hopped out of the car. "Thanks so much for everything today! I owe you."

Daisy gave me a warm smile as I turned around. "Wait!" I turned back as she reached for something in the back seat. She pulled out a stuffed animal from the collection she had won and handed it to me. "It reminded me of you, so you should have it." I grabbed it from her hands and placed it under my arm with a smile.

I turned back and headed toward my door while fishing my key out of my pocket. I looked over my shoulder before I stepped inside my house to see that she was waiting for me to get inside. I did a half wave and shut the door behind me as she drove off.

I kicked off my *Converse* at the door and pulled my phone out as I headed toward the stairs. As I was passing the living room, I noticed my mother sitting in her usual chair. It was her favorite chair, but she had been sitting in it much more often. I found it a bit strange, but I didn't pay any mind to it. She wore a shawl over her and grasped it tightly.

"Why are you wearing that?" I asked her.

She sat up in the chair and turned toward me. "Your father just turned the AC up a lot." The AC wasn't on.

She grinned at me. "But how was your day today?" she asked.

I tried not to smile. "It was fun." With that, I turned and headed upstairs.

I hung my brown flannel on a hook and threw myself on my bed. I looked at my phone and checked the calendar. "Forty-three days of summer left," I said to myself. Though it sounded like a lot, it wasn't at all.

From the Fourth of July, the summer seemed to go by fast. Daisy eventually stopped coming for dinner because her mom came back to town, though that didn't stop her from coming to the café almost every day or even to my house to hang out. But before I knew it, school was starting again.

III

Start to a New School Year

The sun rose again on the day of August seventeenth, the day I started junior year. I rolled out of bed and started getting ready. I couldn't believe that summer was over already.

My brother would be going off to college in two weeks, and I would be taking over the café.

I reached into my closet and pulled out my dry-cleaned uniform. It was yet another year of this stupid uniform. I slipped on my navy-blue skirt and buttoned my white-collared shirt. I then fastened my red tie and glided my arms into my navy-blue-and-red blazer. I turned to look at myself in the mirror and gagged at my appearance. The uniform was tacky and felt ill-fitting with my style. I sighed, grabbed my knee-high socks, and walked downstairs.

The house was quiet, almost too quiet. I turned my head as I passed the living room. My mother sat on her armchair with her head slightly leaning back. Did she sleep there the whole night?

I walked over to her and gently shook her arm. "Mom, it's morning. You should head back to your room."

Her head tilted slowly, and her brown eyes stared back at me. "Did I fall asleep here?" she asked.

I nodded my head. "Yes, you should head back upstairs to your room," I said as I tugged her arm softly.

She stood up and tightened the shawl that resided upon her shoulders. "I think I'll sleep in the bedroom down here for a bit," my mother mumbled before heading past the kitchen.

There was a bedroom just off the dining room; we considered it our guest room, though as of late, my mother had been using it as an art studio. So by now, the floors were cluttered with both finished and unfinished works.

I turned and began walking toward the door. I kneeled and slipped on my socks and shoes. I looked back at the quiet house before walking out. Usually, my father or mother would see me out, but hey, I guess that's growing up for you. I finally slipped my backpack on my shoulders and began walking down the street.

It was such a quiet yet cloudy morning. It was so quiet that I could hear my shoes clicking against the pavement particularly well. I reached into my pocket for my phone and debated about texting Daisy.

In the end, I didn't. I figured that she was running around trying to get her things together. She was up late last night binging shows because, in her words, "Summer isn't over until you fall asleep on the final night."

I sat down on the weathered train station bench and popped my earbuds in my ears. The train wasn't gonna be here for another ten minutes. I began scrolling through webcomics and reading the latest chapters as music roared through my earbuds.

Before I knew it, the train screeched into the station and came to a staggering halt. I stood up and tossed my backpack on only one of my shoulders. The doors opened, and the night shifters scurried off with their usual dead faces.

"School already, Eden?" a voice said behind me. I turned to see a woman in a bright-red blazer and a black shirt with gold accents; it was Ms. Veronica Berimore. She was a neighbor of mine and a frequent customer in the shop.

"What's with the choice of clothing?" I asked while stepping into the train.

She crossed her arms and flicked her blonde highlighted hair. "I have a job!"

I turned and looked in shock. "A job? Didn't you just graduate college?"

She gave a snarky smile. "It was offered to me before I graduated. It's a full-time job!"

I smiled at her. I was proud.

From there we went our separate ways. She went upstairs, and I stayed downstairs where I found an empty row of seats.

The train began moving as I sat down. The once stagnant scenery began to look as if it was moving. I leaned back and placed my earbuds into my ears once more. I closed my eyes as the sun hit my face like a warm embrace.

I must've dozed off for a second because I was jolted awake by a woman tapping my shoulder. "Uh, miss, this is the last stop." I grabbed my book bag and stood up before thanking the kind woman.

I stood by the doors, waiting for them to open. It was crowded with all the working businesspeople and students. I tried to separate myself from the crowd. There was nothing I hated more than crowded tight spaces.

Just then, the doors opened and everyone began to push and shove until they got off the train. I stopped for a moment on the platform and caught my breath. I pulled up my falling school socks and began walking.

My school wasn't too far from the station. It was maybe a twenty-minute walk at most. The sidewalks of downtown were crowded, but I just kept my head down and listened to my music.

As I walked, I saw a variety of uniforms, all different colors. As I got closer to my school, the uniforms began getting more familiar. I had finally reached the school gates when I felt a tap on my shoulder.

I turned to see the gate monitor giving me a stern look. He gestured to his ears. "Headphones…" I quickly pulled them out of my ears and shoved them into my pocket. "How many times have we been over this, Eden? I'm gonna let it go today because it's the first day." I nodded my head and looked back at him. "Look, I'm not the rule maker, just the enforcer. Just don't let it happen again."

I nodded again, "I understand."

I turned and began walking further into the schoolyard. Everyone started looking at me and whispering. I felt my breathing get heavier as I tried to hide my face. I was soon reminded who I was in society. I was the weird, quiet, immigrant kid whom everyone avoided.

I took my eyes off the ground for a split second to see Daisy. She stood with her group of friends huddled in a little circle. She looked at me and gave a little wave. I gave a half wave before putting my head back down. Daisy's friends glared at me before ushering her away.

It became clear to me that Daisy and I lived in completely different worlds. Two worlds that shouldn't collide.

The bell chimed, and everyone began walking into the school. I took one last breath of the city air. "It's gonna rain," I mumbled before heading into the building.

The school building was old, and I was surely surprised that it hadn't fallen yet. It was one of the oldest schools in Chicago but had since then fallen far from its prestigious name.

The school was dark, like a Gothic cathedral. It was surely shocking because of all the windows it had. The hallways always creeped me out; there were paintings of previous prestigious men who walked our very halls. They glare at you judgmentally with their eyes that seem to follow you. The halls usually give off the smell of moldy water and dust, which was different today. On this particular day, they gave off the obnoxious smell of floor wax. Maybe they were trying to be a bit more presentable?

That word only means looking acceptable. The truth was that the school had no air conditioning or working heating. The bathrooms were old and outdated.

I'm going to stop myself right here; my list could go on forever, but it won't change anything. My school would rather fund the sports teams than fix the theater where most students excel and the school gets its name. Okay, that's it. I'm done speaking on this matter.

Where my locker was, I was required to walk across the courtyard into the second building. I opened the door and began walking down the curved path. I stopped for a moment and peered up at the familiar statue. It was of our late president Abraham Lincoln, the man who the school was named after. I turned back to the path and began waking again.

I pushed open the doors of the second building and was hit in the face by the smell of cheap Italian cologne. I knew exactly who the smell was coming from.

"Well, if it isn't Eden!"

I turned to see a boy grinning arrogantly with his gelled hair and cuff pins. My eyes got wide, and I almost choked. "What do you want, Joey?"

He scoffed in my face. "No need to be so rude." He turned to his friends, "Maybe she's mad that her uniform doesn't come in black and white stripes?" Joey's friends behind him began laughing hysterically.

I don't get how his friends find his poor humor hilarious. It's just Joey making a bland joke about a completely unseasoned stereotype. Like that one hasn't been said many times before. While they were laughing, I turned and began sneaking toward my locker.

I took a look at its metal door. You could see the layers of paint on it. It had been repainted many times before. The administrators called it a "random act of vandalism," but I knew it was directed toward me. Then even in the end, they "couldn't find who did it."

I reached into my backpack and pulled out my new set of notebooks and textbooks before putting them on the shelves. In my hands, I kept the books that I needed for the morning.

"Who said that our conversation was over?" Joey said while slamming the books out of my hand. I stood still as everyone looked at me. I covered my ears as I could almost hear the mocking.

"Leave her alone, Joey!" a voice shouted. Then, from the congested hallway, came Daisy. Joey paused as she passed him. Everyone knew that he liked her. Then again, who didn't like Daisy Harrow?

She reached down and began to pick up the fallen books. It gave me a slight sense of déjà vu. I knelt next to her and picked up the rest of the books. Daisy handed them to me and smiled.

Joey looked around awkwardly. "Hey! Daisy, do you wanna—"

She glared at him. "Save it." With that, he scurried away with his friends shortly behind him.

Daisy reached her hand out to me. "Don't let those jerks get to you. They're gone now, but I can't promise that they won't come back." I nodded, and she gave me that familiar smile. "Let me see your schedule." I reached into my folder and pulled out a printed slip of paper. Daisy scooted closer to me and compared it to hers. "We have almost all our classes together!"

I took a peek at her schedule too. "Yeah, including study as well." She had a big grin on her face, and I knew that I was in for it this year.

"C'mon let's walk to first period together!" I smiled and reorganized my books before following her.

We walked down the sunlit hallway side by side. Daisy then glanced over to me. "Are you thinking of doing any extracurriculars?"

I took a moment to think. "I'm not sure. It's a lot of hours, and I got the café to tend to."

Daisy bumped me. "Oh, c'mon! We can do something together. It's our last year to have fun! And plus, you never know if something is gonna be your last!"

I thought again for another moment. "Maybe."

She smiled so genuinely. "Thank you."

I bumped her back. "That doesn't mean I'll actually do it."

Daisy laughed. "Well, 'maybe' means that there's still a possibility!"

We rounded the corner, and I caught a glimpse of Daisy's friend group. I paused and stopped walking any further. "Here, go ahead of me! I just remembered I had to do something."

I saw her surprised face for a moment as I turned and ran off. I figured that it was for the better. She should be with her friends and not someone like me. I turned and walked into the bathroom two hallways away. The place was filled with girls doing their makeup and checking how they look.

I leaned against the wall and pulled out my phone with my free hand. The time was still ten minutes until class. A girl who was applying lip gloss looked over in my direction with a dour look. I quickly slipped my phone back into my pocket. And she shoved the lip gloss applicator back into the tube.

"Stay the hell away from Daisy Harrow. Don't let this morning go to your head. She's not your friend."

I kicked off the wall and rolled my eyes as I turned toward the bathroom door. "Please, you don't have to worry. Nothing is going on."

I was about to leave when the girl grabbed my wrist. "I mean it. Don't ruin things for her, you street rat!"

Usually, I would cower up, but she went too far. I swallowed the nauseating feeling of confrontation and looked her directly in the eyes. "I would rather be a street rat than some stuck-up bitch."

She released my wrist and stood stunned as I left the bathroom. I covered my mouth as I walked down the hall. I didn't think I had it in me. That nausea I swallowed soon came back.

I stopped in front of a large window and peered out. I placed my hands over my ears and took a deep breath. "They can't hurt you anymore." I mumbled to myself before regaining my composure.

I eventually took my eyes off the graying sky and approached the classroom. Daisy was chatting with her friends. They were all laughing and smiling. And I admit, my heart sank a bit.

The teacher tapped me on the shoulder. "Eden." He picked up a sheet of paper and squinted his eyes. "Your seat is…over there." He reached his arm up and pointed his finger to the furthest seat on the left side of the class. I nodded and started walking over.

As I passed Daisy's group, she looked over at me. She had this somber look in her eyes, but it was soon gone as she turned her head.

When I got to my seat, I placed my books on the old wooden desk. You could see the remnants of generations past through the deep carvings and pencil marks from years ago. My desk was right by the windows, the very same ones that shake in the cool Chicago winds. I pulled the chair out and tucked my skirt as I sat. The sky was turning grayer and cloudier by the second.

Mr. Woods turned toward the chalkboard and, with cursive, wrote his name. "For anyone new, welcome, and for everyone else, welcome back." I quickly glanced back toward the window. Outside, the gloomy sky began to drip. From a drizzle to a hard downpour.

I took out a notebook and flipped it to the back. On it, I wrote "History" and flipped it open. I began jotting down the itinerary that the teacher was writing down on the board. Daisy had glanced over at me a few times but quickly turned back.

Soon the familiar old bell echoed throughout the school. Everyone began standing up and gathering their things. Mr. Woods scrambled around, sorting papers. "All right, guys! Remember to write me a brief paper on your favorite historical site. It's due by the end of this week!" He shouted as everyone left, but nobody listened.

I was about to walk out of the classroom door when the teacher stopped me. "Oh, Eden, hold on. It's your lucky day!" I turned toward him slowly.

Here's the thing about Mr. Woods: When he says something's "lucky," it never is.

"Yeah, what's up?" From his podium, he pulled out a slip of paper with a grin. "You've been chosen for dean duty for this semester!"

I snatched the paper with the most dead-set face. "Just what I wanted."

Mr. Woods continued to organize papers. "Look, nobody wants this job, and I get it. But you're the only one who is, well, uh, capable."

I knew the exact reason he picked me. This job destroys friendships, and, well, I barely had any. This job is exactly as it sounds. You're a little assistant to the school dean. That means handing out dress code violation slips, tardy notices, detention slips, and suspension notices, you get the point.

I left the classroom and glared at the slip as I walked. It read "Mandatory start date: August eighteenth." I took a deep breath and crumpled the paper in my right hand. "Tomorrow."

By now it was raining so hard that each drop would make a little click on the old windows. The clicking of my school shoes against the freshly waxed floor was in perfect sync with the rain. It made me feel like I was the only person in the hall. I felt at peace, but peace never lasts.

As I was walking, I felt my right foot get caught on something. Before I knew it, I was falling. My hands and knees hit the floor like a crash of thunder, and my books scattered across the hall. I looked up to see people gathered around me, smiling and laughing with their phones pointed at me.

I turned to see Joey grinning. "You should watch where you're going, little boy!" I knew that he had done it. He acts like a stereotypical high school jock in some teen book. And most of all, he jumps at any chance to mock my short hair.

I reached around to grab all my books, but the whispering and laughing wouldn't stop. I felt my breathing starting to speed up. *Not here!* I thought to myself.

I quickly got up and ran to the nearest bathroom. I locked the stall door and sat down on the toilet. No matter how much air I sucked in, none seemed to go into my lungs. Tears began falling from my eyes slowly. I quickly reached into my pocket and pulled out a pill container. I took out an anxiety pill and swallowed it dry.

I waited for my breathing to calm, and I wiped the tear lines off my cheeks. I sat still and quietly for a moment. Sometimes I hated myself.

This school was for the rich, and I was only here on a scholarship. Maybe I didn't belong? I flushed the empty toilet and walked out of the stall. A few girls remained in the bathroom, so I washed my hands before walking out.

The halls were empty, and I understand that since it was minutes after the bell. My second period this year was Study.

I walked into the quiet room, and the study monitor gave me a mean look. She motioned her finger to have me go to her. "Why are you ten minutes late?" she questioned. I looked around the room and then at her box-dyed red hair. "I had stomach issues…"

Her face changed quickly. "Just go sit down."

I glanced around the room once more to see Daisy. She waved toward me, but I pretended that I didn't see her. I, instead, sat down at an empty table.

I opened my laptop and plugged in my earbuds. I played music as I started writing my history paper.

The chair next to me began scooting out, and the corresponding earbud was taken out of my ear. I turned to see Daisy sitting next to me. Her light eyelashes glowed in the sunlight over her dejected eyes.

"Did I do something wrong?" she asked quietly.

I was caught off guard. I didn't mean to make her feel guilty for anything. I hugged her and whispered over to her, "No! Never!"

I pulled back from the hug and gripped her shoulders. Daisy smiled as tears started to fall from her eyes. I froze as a painful, guilty feeling rushed through my body. I had never seen her cry, let alone cry because of me purposely ignoring her.

I dried her tears carefully with my sleeve. "Don't cry!" I whispered.

Daisy sighed. "I'm just so glad."

I also gave a small smile before handing her the other earbud. She leaned her head on my right shoulder.

"So what historical site are you doing for the history paper?" I asked.

She thought for a moment. "I was thinking maybe Stonehenge in Wiltshire, England. What are you thinking?"

"I'm gonna do the Colosseum in Rome."

Daisy jumped up. "Wait! Rome completely slipped my mind."

I smiled. "Hey, Stonehenge is pretty cool too. Isn't it related to like early witches, magic gates, and ceremonies?"

Daisy nodded her head. "That's why I like it. It's like all mythical!" She started giggling excitedly.

Her nose was still red, just ever so slightly. But her smile distracted me from the fact that she was even crying at all. She just went on about historical sites that were associated with magic or other supernatural phenomena.

After this, the morning seemed to fly by quickly. I gathered my things as the all-school lunch bell began to ring. My school did lunch a bit differently. Instead of separating lunch into multiple periods or grade levels, they had one big all-school lunch that lasted the equivalent of two normal periods. Most kids rush to the lunchroom to beat the long lunch lines, chill in the lounge, or eat in the courtyard; some even nap.

I did none of these. Rather, I spent my lunch in the library. I was on good terms with the librarian, Mrs. Mig, so in return, she would let me eat there. I wouldn't even eat in the lunchroom if you paid me. It's so crowded and dense. The last time I stepped in there, I felt like I was being suffocated, not to mention the soup incident either.

I picked up my books off the desk as I could feel the stampede of students running to lunch. Daisy and her friends stood at the front of the English classroom. They laughed so loud that I could practically taste what they were talking about.

Daisy then looked at me with a sweet smile. "Oh, hey, Eden! Do you wanna join us for lunch in the courtyard?" Her friends turned to her and gave the most "what the hell" look I'd ever seen.

"Why would you invite *her*?"

"Yeah! She's weird."

"I can practically still smell the soup on my uniform!"

Daisy's friends dragged her away and left before she could even get another word in.

A part of me did want to eat lunch with her, but not with those friends of hers. If you can even call them her friends. I just quietly stood up and walked down the empty halls to my locker.

I reached into my backpack and felt around for my lunch. I was soon greeted by the realization that it wasn't there. I took a deep breath. "Well, isn't this great?" I, instead, just walked to the library empty-handed.

It was down the old hallway; it felt almost secret. The old hall was filled with abandoned classrooms and dorms that looked as if they were frozen in time. It was almost creepy. You could see the beautiful original woodworking that began rotting from water damage; it was sad. Nobody truly knew why it was abandoned. I'd heard various rumors from budget cuts to murders.

By the time I was done thinking, I had reached the large, solid wood library doors. They stood so lively in the dead-like hallway. I pushed open the heavy door and was greeted by the comforting smell of oak and ink on paper.

"Well, if it isn't Eden!" a voice exclaimed. I turned to see the dear old librarian smiling sweetly.

"Long time no see, Mrs. Mig!" I laughed.

She paused for a moment. "Now, where is your lunch, sweetheart?"

I looked down at my hands before letting out a light laugh. "I sorta forgot it. But it's whatever."

She stopped me. "You know it's not whatever! I know how early you get up to catch the train, dear. Not once have I ever heard that you ate breakfast." Mrs. Mig then reached for something under her desk. Out came a blue basket decorated with an assortment of collected stickers. It was filled to the top with snacks like crackers, granola bars, and cookies. Mrs. Mig winked at me and gestured toward the said bucket. "Don't be shy, sweetheart." I smiled and grabbed a pack of crème-filled cookies.

I sat down at my usual seat. It was a big desk in the far back of the library. Mrs. Mig always questioned why I chose such a faraway seat if the library was so empty at this time. I just answered her, "Well, it's the perfect seat."

This quiet time gave me the chance to finish my history paper. I was left with so much time that I began writing a story.

I had written short stories before and of how much I liked them; it was weird that I hadn't written a book yet. So I opened a new document and placed a title, "A Place to Be on Summer Nights." The words seemed to flow as I wrote my thoughts into words, and words into sentences.

I had finished a chapter or two before the period was over. I waved Mrs. Mig goodbye, and I headed off to class.

The afternoon usually went by fast. Before I knew it, the final bell rang. Kids rushed to their lockers and more out the door. Everyone tried to rush to the school café before they ran out of strawberry lemonade. I found no joy in overly sweet concoctions that are marked up double their value. So I simply gathered my things and left.

As I was heading out the gate, I heard light footsteps rushing toward me. I turned around to see Daisy. She appeared out of breath, and her hair was slightly a mess. In one of her hands, though, was the cup of the strawberry lemonade I was just talking about.

"You need to slow down!" I reached my hands out and fixed her hair. "And you need to stop wasting money on practically sugar and water."

Daisy smiled. "But I got something for you too!" From behind her back, she pulled out a mocha frappe. "It was a new menu item. I thought that you would like it!"

I grabbed it from her hands and gave her a cynical look. "Why are you really getting me this?" Daisy began fidgeting with her fingers that were around the cup of her lemonade. "Um…I wanted to apologize for my friends and for today. I heard about your run-ins earlier, and I just felt so bad—"

I put my hand on her head and smiled. "There is no reason for you to be so sorry for it. I know how everyone is already." With a saddened smile from her, we began walking to the station.

In my mind, I was screaming out. It was painful to excuse such horrible people. Then again, I'd let it happen. They were her friends and schoolmates, plus we lived in completely different worlds. Though it bugged me for the longest time. They never really seemed like her friends. Like fakes who still hold onto her for bites of popularity.

Under all that regurgitated kindness and fake eyelashes were nothing but snakes. The kind of snake who would drop someone the moment their status falls. But Daisy was too nice, too nice for her own good. And most of all, too nice to see. But who am I to tell her?

IV

Conversation to Overhear

Tell me, what's the difference between nice people and the ones who pretend to be? Well, if you think about it, not much at all. One is just nice, while the other holds malice deep in their heart.

But there is one key detail to set them apart. The fake would do anything to keep up their image. Take that away and the house of cards falls.

But who was I to be playing with cards? So I let the house stand and walked away.

However, sometimes cards shift, knocking the whole house over. I didn't think it would happen so soon, until I stumbled upon a conversation that I was not meant to hear.

I believe it was a Friday, a bit over a week after I started dean duty. I found that it wasn't all too bad. It was only forty minutes out of my lunch, and I found that it was a good workout. Sure, it comes with its handful of profanity that gets thrown at you, but that's a given.

You would think, "Hey it's the beginning of the school year. Your job should be easy!" You'd be surprised.

Just on my first day, I handed out five detentions and nearly ten dress code violations. It makes me kinda paranoid; these teachers must really care about being in uniform.

I also remember on this day in particular, there was a surplus of slips that the dean needed to hand out. So I was asked if I could go after school and stick them onto lockers. I didn't mind, it was only gonna take me a few minutes.

After the final bell rang, I stopped at my locker to put all my books in my backpack and slipped the said bag onto my shoulders.

After that, I walked the long hall to the dean's office. My school's layout was weird, to say the least. There was only one hallway you could use to get to the administration offices. It was long, narrow, and smelled like a dingy basement.

The hall was always quiet and eerie. You could hear the subtle scraping of your shoes on the old carpeting. It was always oddly comforting for some reason.

I eventually came across the final door in the hall, the dean's office. I knocked twice on the wooden door and was let in by the dean. "I'm here to report for duty, Mr. Taylor."

He looked at me as he grabbed his shoulder bag, "Oh, hello, Eden!"

He then pulled out a paper-looking bag from behind his desk. "Everything should be sorted in this bag. And as for locker numbers…" Mr. Taylor then pulled a paper off his desk and handed it to me. It gave a long list of locker numbers and their corresponding slip. Some read "dress code"; others read "behavior violation." Some even were dean or councilor summons.

Mr. Taylor put on his hat and tapped it into place. "Please don't worry about your duty next week."

I turned toward him as I shoved the sheet into the bag. "Is there a reason as to why?"

He smiled before walking out the door. "My husband and I are going on vacation!" I watched him walk out with a pep in his step. I was happy for him, but the second week of school was just kinda pushing it. That was quite a weird time to go on vacation.

I made sure everything was in the bag before heading out. The first locker to go to was C44. I walked over and posted the sheet on the locker door and moved on. From C44 to C56 and on.

While I was in hallway E, I stumbled into someone familiar. "Daisy?" She walked with her backpack on one of her shoulders as she sorted a stack of papers.

She looked up at me. "Eden? Why are you still here?" I lifted the locker sheet that was in my hand. "I'm on dean duty, but I could ask you the same thing."

Daisy then slipped the papers into a folder as she talked. "I was just getting class materials for Susana. She's a student who went home early."

I looked down at the locker sheet. I only had about five lockers left to pay a visit to. "Wanna walk with me? I've only got a few left."

Daisy shoved the folder into her backpack. "Of course! Let me just get this in before I lose a paper or something." She then caught up to me, and we started walking together.

We talked about random things, like how she bought a new plant or how I found another good book series. I even let her post a few notices on lockers. I, of course, made sure nobody was around.

We finally made our way to hallway G. "Okay, this is the last one." I took out the last slip from the bag and stuck it onto the locker. "And that's it!" I folded up the bag, and we started to head back toward hallway A.

Daisy looked at me. "Aw! I just remembered. I'm not gonna be able to go to your house today for dinner."

I turned to her. "Really! That sucks. My dad is making soufflé for dessert."

Daisy grabbed my arms. "Please save me one!"

I softly laughed. "I promise I will. Just stop by—"

Daisy suddenly stopped walking and put her arm in front of me.

"What's going on?" I whispered.

She fell silent and just stood still. Then I heard it.

A group of girls were talking just around the corner. I could make out a few people's voices. Rose, then there was Sarah, and Nova too; they were Daisy's friends. I leaned against the wall and tried to listen in.

"Daisy's running down our reputation. She needs to stop hanging out with that ugly bitch."

"What is with Daisy anyway? She thinks she's better than all of us or something, with her exhausting kindness act."

"Right! Is she actually nice or just plain stupid? Either way, she annoys the shit out of me."

"I don't know about you guys, but I'm only putting up with her crap because she's popular and rich. Her blinding kindness is a perk too, remember. She thinks we're her friends, so she feels obligated to buy us shit."

I tried to cover Daisy's ears as the girls started laughing, but I think I was too late.

She pushed my hands off her ears and walked around the corner. I followed shortly behind her. Daisy's expression was blank as she walked up to the girls.

"Is that what you actually think of me?" The girls' faces shifted quickly from judgmental scowls to nervous smiles.

Nova stepped forward. "Daisy! What are you doing here? I thought you went home already?" The girls stared at me, but they didn't dare comment about my presence at this moment.

"Are you guys even my friends?" Daisy asked them.

Sarah stepped forward and grabbed her hands. "Of course, we are!"

Even though she said this, Daisy didn't spare a moment. "What's my favorite color?"

I even knew that it was—

"Purple!"

Daisy whipped her hands away and started laughing. "If you guys were gonna fake being my friends for three years, at least learn something about me first."

Sarah acted as if this was a huge shock to her. "When did you change it? It's always been purple!"

Daisy sighed before turning around. "Just for your knowledge, it's always been yellow." She grabbed my wrist and started walking.

Rose finally spoke as we walked away. "Just so you know, you're nothing without us!"

Daisy glared back. "I would rather be nothing than have nothing."

Silence fell for a moment before Rose spoke again. "And what about her? How can you be so sure that she's not here to ride your popularity train? I doubt that she's actually your friend either!"

I turned around this time. I was fed up with their crap. Something in me snapped again, like in the bathroom that one day. "I am more of a friend than you guys will ever be to her! You guys never gave a shit about Daisy! At least I care!" Their faces were stuck in an expression of pure shock. Not another word slipped out from their lips. I turned back and grabbed Daisy's wrist before walking to the building exit.

Daisy didn't speak a word the whole way to the doors. Rather, a contemplative silence filled the void. I didn't look back at her; we just kept walking like Orpheus and Eurydice.

I wanted to ask so many things. I wanted to tell her that it was all gonna be okay. I wanted to tell her sorry, but I don't think I could say that. In truth, I wasn't sorry. I'm glad she witnessed the true colors of those girls.

I stopped walking when we got to the school gates. I turned to her. "Are you okay?"

Daisy's lips were tightly pressed together as tears ran down her face. "Oh! I'm sorry! I don't know why I'm crying. I'm such a baby, aren't I?" She laughed.

I don't know what came over me at that moment, but everything just spilled out. I pulled her closer and gently hugged her. "It's okay. Cry as much as you want." She cried a bit more before eventually calming down. I wiped the tears off her face. "See, don't you feel better now?"

Daisy nodded her head. "I just feel so betrayed. But I'm also glad that I see the truth now."

She nervously bit her lip. "I'm so sorry I didn't stand up for you properly today and earlier this week. I'm starting to realize that I'm not that good of a friend."

I put my hand on her head. "Don't sweat it. You're an amazing friend to me, and you always will be." She smiled at me, and we started walking down the sidewalk.

Just then, Daisy's phone chimed. After looking at it, she let out a big sigh.

"What's wrong?" I asked.

"My plans fell through. My mom has to fly back to New York for some last-minute business agreement or something. She doesn't want me to be alone in the condo anymore."

I thought for a second. "Well, you could sleep over at my place," I suggested.

Daisy pointed her finger at me. "Yes! But wait, you've never had a sleepover before, have you?"

I shook my head no. I could tell by the look on her face that she was planning something. "What are you planning to do, Daisy?"

She just laughed. "I can't tell you yet!" She glanced at her phone and thought for a second. "I'll be over at six. I'll see ya!" Daisy then ran off before I could say bye.

She seemed so happy, but I knew deep down that she was hurting. Anyone would be after finding out your friends of three years were just using you the whole time. Maybe this sleepover would be good for her. It's something to distract her from all of this. Everything that happened today had gotten me to rethink some things.

You would think people on two different social levels lived in completely different worlds. That wasn't so much the case anymore. Because what happened to Daisy had already happened to me years ago. It's the one reason why I didn't have any friends or rather didn't want any. I was so sure that I never wanted friends again.

But somehow, here I was. I was on a train going home to get ready to have a sleepover. It seemed childish, but it was something I never got to experience. I was so happy that I didn't notice the smile on my face when I walked into the house.

"What's got you all smiley? It looks weird on you, E'ed."

I turned to see Louis lugging a box through the kitchen. I wiped the smile off my face, "Well, what are you doing? You look weirder."

He stood up and clapped his hands. "I'm heading down for college on Sunday. Did you forget?"

I gave him a look as I took off my shoes. "I didn't forget. I just lost track of the day, that's all."

Louis gave me a grin as he placed his hand on my shoulder. "Aw, you're gonna miss me so much, aren't you?"

I pushed his hand off. "You wish."

Even though I said that, Louis was right. I was gonna miss him even if I never said it.

"Eh, it was worth a shot. Oh, but you know what?"

I sat down on the island stool. "What?"

He pointed toward me. "You…are gonna run the café from now on. That means even putting in the supply orders."

I leaned forward. "Why can't Dad do it? What does he do all day?"

Louis thought for a moment. "Dad does…Dad things, I guess."

I gave him a dissatisfied look. "Whatever."

Louis looked at the boxes then back at me. "Can you give me a hand?"

"No," I said, not even letting him finish.

"What are you even doing right now?" he asked.

"Eden things." I grinned before going up the stairs.

I threw myself on my bed. "A sleepover, huh?" I mumbled to myself. I grabbed my phone and searched "What to do on a sleepover."

"Hang out in hammocks? Play outside? Take Fido for a walk?" I said as I sat up. "I don't know if this was meant for rich people or eight-year-olds. And who the hell is Fido?" Either way, I knew one thing: I didn't know how to entertain. This sleepover was going to be awkward.

I looked back at my phone. "Do each other's makeup, prank call, talk about crushes?" It was a word I hadn't heard in a while, *crush*. It's one of those words that gets tossed around in middle school or in books written by teenagers. It made me think for a moment, *What really is a crush?*

I once again turned toward my phone. "Compress or squeeze forcefully to break or distort the shape of something? Gosh, I hope not!" I looked a bit further. "The infatuation with someone to where you want to date them." I don't know if I've ever felt like that. Is there something wrong with me?

I scrolled even further and found a site of anonymous confessions.

> There is this person in my history class. I really like them! Every time they talk to me, I get butterflies! They don't see me as a potential match, though. This person has so much experience, and I'm scared to put myself out there because I've only ever dated one person before.

I read more and more, and I felt even more like an outsider than ever before. I finally put down my phone. "I'm thinking way into this."

I got off my bed and changed out of my uniform. I reached up on my closet shelf for the air mattress, but it wasn't there. I ran downstairs and peeked into the living room. "Mom, have you seen the air mattress?"

She sat in her armchair and looked over at me. "I threw it away. It was old and had holes in it." Crap. "Why are you suddenly asking about an air mattress?"

I sighed. "Daisy is sorta staying over…" I tightened my fingers; it completely slipped my mind to ask her first.

"Well, your bed is big enough. She'll just have to sleep with you."

"W-with me?" I swallowed.

"You guys are both girls, so it's fine."

I clapped my hands together. "Right! Okay, thank you." I walked away, shocked that a sleepover flew right over her head. Maybe that's a sign I've had Daisy over too much.

I lit a few candles in my room as six rolled around. The doorbell eventually rang, and I sprinted down the stairs. "Slow down!" my mom shouted from the living room. I opened the door to see Daisy.

She wore a bag across her shoulders and yellow canvas shoes hidden by her baggy pants. She grabbed my shoulders.

"Are you ready for the best night of your life?" She grinned.

I didn't know how great this night could be. In truth, every night with Daisy was the best of my life. "We'll just have to see."

We ran up to my room after having dinner. My father had even made Daisy extra dessert. I swear sometimes he likes Daisy better than he likes me.

On my bedroom floor, she opened up an unfolding box. It had layers on layers and looked as if it could hold so much! "Step one in giving you the great sleepover experience, a makeover!"

Now, I'd never done makeup until now, so I was clueless about what she was doing. She dabbed my face with a bit of something and a bit of another thing. She grabbed my hair in her hands and tied little pigtails. "And done!"

I turned toward the mirror and burst out laughing. "Besides the pigtails, I look good."

Daisy pulled the hair ties out. "I worked so hard on those!"

I grabbed her hand. "No, put them back."

She looked at me. "But I thought you didn't like them?"

I smiled. "I meant that they looked dumb. That doesn't mean I don't like them." She paused for a moment and tied my hair up again.

"Okay! It's your turn to give me a makeover now."

I put my hand on her head. "You don't need makeup. You're beautiful as is."

Daisy grabbed my hand and held it in hers. "Y-You're just saying that because you don't know how to do makeup."

I grinned. "The compliment is sincere, not being able to do makeup is a bonus."

She stood up. "Well, next we could make a fort, watch a movie, eat snacks, or—"

I grabbed her hand. "You don't have to try so hard for me. I know you wanna give me a good experience, but it's good sometimes to take it one step at a time. Besides, I wanna show you something."

I walked over to the window and opened it up.

"What are you doing?" she asked.

"You'll see," I said as I hopped out the window.

"Eden!" she screamed. Daisy ran to the window and looked out just to see me sitting on the roof.

"You bastard! I thought you were dead!"

I gasped jokingly. "Is the great Daisy Harrow calling me a bastard?"

"Just don't do that again, you ass!"

I laughed and raised my hand. "So will you join me, princess?" She grabbed my hand, and I helped her down to the roof.

"Who are you and where is Eden?" she said. It made me think back to what my mom said, *"Promise that you'll take care of that girl. She brings out a part of you that you locked away years ago."* She was completely right. For once, I felt like me and not a shell of someone who once was. A more confident person, someone who wouldn't get pushed around.

I handed Daisy a blanket, and we sat against the house wall. "Look, you can see some stars!" she pointed. Daisy then folded her hands and closed her eyes. She nudged me. "Aren't you gonna make a wish?"

I folded my hands and closed my eyes, "I wish for abundant wealth!"

She nudged me again. "That's not how it works!"

I leaned over. "Well then, what did you wish for?"

Daisy opened her eyes. "You can't tell someone a wish! It won't come true that way."

I sighed. "Fine!" I then leaned my head onto her shoulder, and we just lay there for a while.

I wanted to ask if she was okay. It was as if today never happened. As if she didn't lose her friends and find out they were fake.

"I'm okay," she said as she ran her fingers through my hair.

I closed my eyes. "I'll believe you for now."

I looked at the sky, then back at her. "Have you ever dated someone?"

She smiled at me. "That was outta nowhere, but nah. I guess I've never found the right *person*."

I thought for a moment. "Well, have you ever had a crush on someone?"

She laughed with her cheeks turning a warm pink. "Huh? Well, uh, yeah."

I grinned. "Well, do you have one right now?"

Her expression dropped, and her face turned beet red. Daisy then shoved my face away from hers. "W-Where are you going with this?"

I smiled and put my hand on her head as she tried to hide her face. "It's okay, I won't push you any further."

I don't know why, but my heart sank. Why was I disheartened that Daisy liked someone? I couldn't possibly have a crush on her, could I?

No, it's not possible.

V

Seasons Change

Time moved on as it always does. Leaves changed from green to warm hues of reds and oranges. And before I knew it, my seventeenth birthday rolled around.

The house smelled sweet as I walked down the stairs.

"October 23rd, skies look clear as temperatures start to dim to 64°. It looks like a nice day to make sweet memories!"

The man spoke on the radio from the kitchen. The sunlight peeked through the windows as my dad cooked.

"Are you making pancakes?" I asked him.

He turned around and tried to cover the stove. "No! Close your eyes!"

I laughed as I sat down at the island. "You don't have to make me birthday pancakes every year, Dad."

He sighed, scooped the last pancakes off the pan, and turned toward me. "Are you tired of our traditions already?"

I shook my head and grabbed candles out of the drawer. "Do you wanna do the honors?" I asked.

My dad smiled, stuck the candles in the pancakes, and lit them. "Happy birthday, darling."

The house felt quiet, and the day was just like any other. It didn't feel like my birthday. Louis left for college, and he couldn't make it today. This would be the first year he would not be here. If you were to ask me about my birthday plans, I would say "*nothing*."

I ate my pancakes as a *happy birthday* text came across my phone. It was from Louis. It was followed by "Hey, E'ed, sorry I couldn't make it. I promise that I will give you an amazing gift next time I see you." I sighed and shut my phone off.

I looked up at my dad. "Do you need help with the café today?"

He looked at me like I was crazy. "But it's your birthday!"

I just smiled at him and said, "It's okay. I'm not doing anything anyway."

After I finished eating, I glanced into the living room before heading up to my room. My mother wasn't sitting in her usual chair. I figured that she was still sleeping.

So there I was, sitting behind a counter, working, on my birthday. I didn't mind, though. Through the cafe, my father was prancing around. Like he was waiting on something. "We don't have any shipments today. What are you waiting for?"

He gave a nervous smile. "Nothing! Just continue doing what you do!" He was acting strange.

"Happy birthday!" a voice said from behind me. I turned to see Daisy. She stood with a teddy bear and balloons.

"How are you here? And behind the counter? I didn't see you come in!"

She laughed. "Your dad let me in through the back."

I soon realized why he was all antsy. I hugged her tightly. "How did you remember my birthday?"

Daisy smiled. "How could I forget?"

My father grabbed the stuff from her as she grabbed my hands. "Let's go!"

I stopped and asked, "Where?"

Daisy sweetly laughed. "It's a secret, idiot." She dragged me out of the café as my dad grinned. I know he planned all of this. He may not look like it, but that man's an evil mastermind, that or he's just French.

I sat down in the passenger seat and put on my seat belt. "Can I get a hint?"

Daisy thought for a moment. "Nope!"

I grinned. "You jerk!"

With that, we drove off. Through the streets, the scenes of houses turned into acres of trees. Then we reached a street of cute old-time-looking buildings. "Okay, we're here!"

I turned to see a sign that read, *Tilley Park Roller Rink*. "We're going roller skating!"

Daisy nodded. "You ever been?" I shook my head. I was never invited to those roller-skating parties, so I'd never been.

We hopped out of the car, and Daisy grabbed a yellow skate bag from the back seat. "This is one of my favorite places," she said as we walked to the entrance.

Through the wooden doors, there was a lobby covered with miscellaneous decorations. A lady behind the pay window lit up. "Daisy! It's been a minute. And you brought a *friend* for once!"

Daisy smiled as she handed her cash. "It's good to see you too, Mrs. Sydney." Daisy handed me an orange rental ticket before busting through the doors that led to the rink.

"Ah! I missed that smell."

I took a deep breath in, but all I could smell were the carpets and the dim scent of pizza, although it was oddly comforting, like that one hall in school.

The concessions area was filled with arcade games and claw machines. Kids on skates zoomed past me, nearly knocking me over. Daisy grabbed my hand. "Be careful." Through the threshold was the skating area. People zoomed by, and some did tricks to the blasting music.

I followed Daisy to the rental booth. "Women's size nine, please." The boy turned and grabbed a pair of skates.

"RJ?" Daisy asked with her face lighting up.

The boy turned back around. "Ay! Daisy! I haven't seen you around!"

Daisy laughed. "I took a small break. Didn't think you'd be working today?" It seemed like she knew everyone. "Oh, RJ, this is Eden."

RJ smiled. "Sup! I'm Ronnie James, a.k.a. RJ. I used to be Daisy's neighbor until her ass got rich and moved away."

I waved my hand. "I'm Eden. I go to school with her."

RJ grinned at Daisy. "I see…"

Daisy grabbed the skates, then my hand, and dragged me away. "I-I'll talk to you later!"

We sat down on the bench, and I gazed out onto the skating floor. People of all different ages sped past me.

Daisy knelt below me. "Give me your foot."

I kicked my foot up, and she slid the skate on. "I-I could do it myself!" I said, covering my face.

"No, it's your birthday," she responded.

My heart started to speed up. *"There's this person I like. And whenever they do the smallest thing for me, my heart speeds up and I get butterflies!"* I recall reading off the Internet. But I just thought, *No! It can't be!*

Daisy finished lacing up the last skate. "Okay, make sure they're not too tight or too loose."

I stood up, and my ankles felt wobbly. "What they feel like is a night at the ER."

Daisy laughed as we started walking over to the floor.

"Are you ready to jump in?"

I looked at all the passing people. "Are you crazy! We're gonna get run over!"

Despite my pleading, she counted, "Three…two…"

I tried pulling back. "Wait! Hold on!"

Daisy grinned, "One!" She yanked my hand, and we flew onto the floor.

The difference between the carpet and the waxed wood floor sent me falling. Daisy grabbed my hip and set me upright. "Be careful!" I think it was a little too late for that. She then pointed down toward her feet. "Kick your feet out like this to move. You never wanna just walk with skates on."

I did as she said and we began moving. "I did it! We're moving!"

Daisy held my hand, and I slowly started getting the hang of it.

"What a nice couple!" RJ had skated from behind us with a cheesy grin.

"RJ!" Daisy shouted before going off to chase him. I watched her go after him like a small child.

Couple. I thought about it for a minute. What did he mean by that? I was so caught up in the thought that I didn't see that the kid in front of me had fallen. I tried to avoid him, but I ended up falling myself.

Daisy rushed over to me. "I'm so sorry! Are you okay?"

I just laughed. "I'm okay!"

She helped me up, and we started again. "Ignore RJ. He can be pretty annoying sometimes."

I nervously bit my lip. "Do you have a crush on him?"

Daisy laughed. "That was out of nowhere! But no, I've known him for so long. He's like a brother to me. An annoying one at that." I felt relieved; it was weird. "Why were you asking? D-Do you like someone?"

I paused. "I don't know."

She smiled. "Well, I hope you figure it out."

We finally sat down, and I rested my feet on the bench. "My feet hurt like hell!"

Daisy laughed at my misery. "I forgot to mention that it would, didn't I?"

I sighed. "You think?"

Daisy looked at her watch and then back at me. "Wanna get milkshakes?" I nodded my head and ripped off the roller skates.

"RJ mentioned that you guys were neighbors. Where did you live before?"

Daisy put the skate bag strap on her shoulder and pointed, "Right over there, behind the rink."

I thought for a moment. "Whoa, that's crazy close to here!"

She nodded. "It was a yellow house with small pillars. Well, now the house is white. But RJ lived right next door to the left. My dad would take us to the rink anytime it was open to skate." Her smile was bright as she talked.

"He must be a really fun guy," I said.

"Yeah," she mumbled.

I returned my skates, and we walked out the door. "So milkshakes?"

Daisy smiled. "There is this really cute diner not far from here. They make the best milkshakes."

I smiled back. "Then let's go."

The diner wasn't far just as she had said. It looked old and preserved. Like it was in a time bubble from the sixties. We got out and sat at the counter with the red bar seats. This place looked exactly like the image that comes to mind when you think of a classic diner. I ordered a chocolate crunch milkshake, and Daisy ordered the strawberry sundae milkshake.

"We are like opposites!"

I gave a confused look. "What do you mean?"

She pointed at me. "Dark." Then she pointed to herself. "Light." Then again, "Day…night" and again, "Sun…moon."

I laughed. "Okay, I get it now."

Daisy shrugged. "I guess opposites do attract."

The waitress walked over and placed the milkshakes in front of us. Daisy lifted her glass. "To your birthday!"

I lifted mine and clinked it against hers. "To my birthday."

Daisy grinned as she took a sip. "Just as good as I remember."

Mine was pretty good too. I'd have to keep this place in mind. "Thanks for this, really."

She looked over. "Oh! No problem. But hasn't anyone done this for you before?" she asked.

I swirled the straw in my drink nervously. "No, I've never really had friends." I took a deep breath and smiled. "And, Daisy, in just the short time that I've known you, you've given me more than any friend has in all seventeen years I've lived." I turned to see Daisy holding back tears.

She hugged me. "Nobody should ever have to go through that. Not experiencing friendship!" She pulled herself out of the hug and grabbed my shoulders. "We're best friends, right?"

I laughed and hugged her again. "Yes, yes we are."

Daisy pulled out her instant camera. "Can we take one?"

I kicked off my shoes at the door and headed toward the stairs. "Eden," my mother called from the living room.

I turned to see her sitting in the usual chair. "Happy birthday, sweetheart. I'm sorry, I lost track of time, and you were gone by the time I got up."

I walked into the living room and sat down. "It's okay, I was with Daisy."

She smiled. "I'm glad."

Before I stood up, I asked, "That doctor's appointment yesterday, how did it go?"

My mother paused for a moment. "Everything is fine."

That line seemed to unsettle me. It seemed almost as if she had lied. In the end, I believed her and headed up to my room.

VI

Lights So Beautiful

The weather got colder, and snow eventually fell. It was yet again another Chicago winter.

Today was December twentieth, the last day of finals. Daisy texted me in the morning, nearly freaking out. She had forgotten to study a whole chapter for her physics final. She's good at the subject, way better than me at least, so I said she would be fine.

I sat on the train station bench as I waited. The ground was covered in snow, so delays were expected. I reached into my pocket and pulled out my earbuds. I untangled the wires and put them in my ears, except when I pressed play on my music, the left speaker went out. "Damn it," I mumbled and ripped them out of my ears.

"Merry Christmas, Eden!" I turned to see Ms. Veronica Berimore. This time she wore a bright-yellow blazer.

"I didn't know there were auditions for the yellow crayon today?"

She huffed. "Well, I got it on sale, and I think it's pretty lovely."

I laughed. "I'm joking."

She looked at me like I had two heads. "Joking?" Veronica placed her hand on my forehead. "Are you sure this cold hasn't given you a fever?"

I pulled her hand off. "I'm perfectly fine."

She smiled at me and took a step back as if she thought it wasn't me. "Well, you've never joked like that before. If it's even you."

I sighed. "My name is Eden Marie Aubert. I have an older brother named Louis, and my family owns a bookstore-cafe."

Veronica started laughing hysterically. "It actually is you, man! What changed in you or rather who?"

I paused. When and what changed in me? Was it her? I smiled. "There's this girl. I've only known her for a few months, but it feels like years."

She put her hand on my shoulder. "It's probably her. I haven't seen you this happy since you were that little energetic neighbor kid. She brings the good out in you." It was just as my mom had said previously. I was thankful for everything Daisy had done for me.

"Hey, Christmas is coming up. Maybe you should give her a nice gift, if you haven't already."

I grinned. "That's perfect!"

The train pulled up to the station, and we got on. I went upstairs and sat by the window and thought. What could I get her? I grabbed my phone and scrolled through social media for ideas. An ad for a ring company came up, and I thought, *That's it! That's what I'll give Daisy.*

The last thing to think of was when to give the gift. She was always taking me places, so what if I took her somewhere for a change? I tried to think of Christmas activities. Ice skating? No. Mall Santa? Definitely not. Zoo lights? Yes! That's perfect. I went online and bought two tickets. I'd add them to her gift. I grinned the rest of the train ride just thinking of her expression.

I hopped off the warm train to the cold city. It was moments like this that made me wish I had a car. I still pushed on walking even if the hood of my coat practically covered my eyes.

"You're not listening to music?"

I turned to see Daisy next to me. "Ah, no. My earbuds actually broke this morning." She nodded and didn't respond.

"Daisy, are you doing anything on Christmas Eve?"

She shook her head. "Nope! My mom's gonna be in LA until the fourth. Why?"

I tried to hide my smile. "I have a gift for you. So meet me at my house at five and don't plan anything." She gave me a thumbs-up and we walked into the schoolyard.

After school, I rushed to get a rideshare. There was an antique store that specialized in old jewelry; it was about a ten-minute drive from the school. Throughout the car drive, I just thought nonstop about how Daisy would react. How her face would light up when she saw the present.

"Ma'am we're here," the driver said.

"Oh! Sorry," I said as I got out.

The antique storefront was just gorgeous. Walking into the store was like walking into another world. "Welcome to Mysteek's Antiques!" a girl said as she dragged a box to the back of the store. "I'll be with you in a moment!" she shouted again. The girl walked from the back room. She had short ash-brown braids and round black glasses that hid her freckles. She rolled up her sleeves. "Okay, how can I help you—" She paused. "Eden?"

Her accent sounded familiar, so I looked at her again. "Chloé?"

The girl started jumping up and down. "It is you!" Standing behind that very counter was my first ever friend.

Back in France, I lived in a tight-knit community; everyone knew each other. Next to my house lived a girl named Chloé. We would hang out at the park, at each other's houses, and in school. But being so young, we lost contact after I moved.

"When did you come to America?" I asked her.

"I moved here three years ago. My Maman got offered a good job down here."

I laughed. "I didn't think I would see you again."

Chloé laughed as well. "Oh, wait, how is your *mère*? I was told you moved because she was sick."

I was shocked that she still remembered. "Oh, thank you. She's doing way better now."

Chloé gasped. "Oh right! You were here to find something!" She still acted the same as she always did.

"I was looking for a ring for someone I know."

She reached behind the counter and pulled out trays of different rings. "We got big ones, small ones, shiny ones, men's ones. Anything you can think of." I took a look at the rows of rings. They were all unique, and none were the same.

I looked up and down, but they didn't quite feel like Daisy. Until I came across one in particular. As soon as I laid my eyes on it, it was like I knew this was the one. It was a beautiful gold ring with a green gem on top. It reminded me of Daisy's eyes. "This one. This is the one."

Chloé took a look at it. "Ah, that one. It's quite beautiful. I believe it's, uh, from the nineteen fifties."

I twisted the ring in my fingers. I was just mesmerized by the twisting pattern.

"Eden?"

I looked up. "Sorry, yes?"

She had put the rest of the trays away. "I was just saying that I can give it to you for twenty-five and gift-wrap it. Is that good?" I nodded my head and handed her the ring.

Chloé went to the back, and when she returned, she had an antique octagon ring box.

"Is the box going to be extra?"

She shook her head. "It had a broken hinge, so my boss was gonna throw it out anyway. Don't worry! I fixed the hinge already." I smiled and paid for the ring.

"We should catch up some time," I said, handing her my phone.

Chloé smiled, "I would like that. I'm free after New Year's, so let me know."

I put the ring in my backpack and headed back toward the train station. I pulled out my phone. I was gonna text Daisy and tell her what happened. But I paused. She would ask why I was at an antique store in the first place. Sure, I could lie, but she always sees through them. I'd tell her later.

The ring box sat on my dresser. It was all I could think about. It's like I became obsessed. I was excited like a small child. I thought about it so much that the time came quickly.

When I looked up, it was already Christmas Eve. I dug through my closet to find something to wear, but no matter what I picked, it just didn't seem good enough.

I ran down the stairs and slid into the living room. "Ma! Pa! I need to go buy new clothes!" They looked at me like I was crazy. "One, it's Christmas Eve. Two, who are you meeting that you wanna dress up nice for?" my mother asked.

"Maybe our baby girl is finally dating someone. Who is he... or she, we don't judge." My father grinned. "D-Dad...no! Whatever, I'll find something."

In the end, I just wore jeans and a band T-shirt under my puffy jacket.

I paced around my room as five rolled around. "Eden! Daisy's here!" my father shouted. I quickly grabbed the gift bag before sprinting down the stairs. "Bye, Dad. See you later!" I quickly said before bolting out of the house.

"You need to slow down. You're gonna fall one day," Daisy said as she fixed my hair. I held out the small gift bag. "Open it, please." She smiled and grabbed the bag from my hands. She reached in and pulled out the ring box and opened it.

She let out a gasp, and her jaw dropped. "Eden, this is...gorgeous. It's like the one my grandma used to have, except hers was red." She slid it on her left ring finger and hugged me. "Oh, Eden, you didn't have to give me anything.

I hugged her back. "There's more."

She looked back in the bag, and her face lit up when she saw the tickets. "The zoo lights!" Daisy jumped around, squealing. I finally got to witness the reaction I was dying to see. "And the day is for today?" she asked.

I nodded. "Yeah, so let's get a move on."

Though there was crazy Christmas Eve traffic, we arrived, and the time was nearing six thirty. By then, the night was in full swing. Daisy grabbed my wrist, "Let's go! I've always wanted to see these!"

Past the gates were tons of light displays. From underpasses of rainbow lights to glowing reindeers. I let Daisy lead the way. She ran around taking pictures. "Can we do this again next year?"

I smiled at her. "As many times as you want."

After getting hot chocolate, we sat down on a bench. "Now, for your present."

I was surprised. "Oh no, you didn't need to get me anything."

She placed a decorative bag in my hand. "But I did anyway."

I reached inside the bag to find a pair of new black headphones. I hugged her. "Oh, thank you so much!"

She smiled softly. "You said that yours broke, so I got you new ones. But there's more."

I reached into the bag again and pulled out a small brown photo album. On the cover were golden outlines of flowers. I opened it to see polaroids of us—the picture she took on the Ferris wheel, to even the picture on my birthday. "I've been collecting the pictures and putting them in here. So that way, we can fill it up with pictures. Oh, and when you fill that one up, I can get you another!"

I smiled. "This means a lot to me."

Daisy reached into her tote bag and pulled out her instant camera. "Let's add one more photo." I leaned my head on her shoulder, and she snapped the photo. "Okay, just wave it until you can see the picture."

I fanned it around, and the photo began showing. "No way! That's so cool."

She then took the photo and slipped it into the book. Daisy stood up and grabbed my hand. "Let's go see more lights!"

VII

New Year—New Changes

Louis had made it home in time for Christmas. He showed up at the door at nine in the morning on Christmas Day. None of us had expected him to come since he had been so busy recently. Louis didn't come empty-handed; rather, he came with a car full of gifts.

"I told you I'd bring you a good gift," he said to me, grinning. His smile made me almost scared. Wouldn't you be scared if your brother, who you haven't seen since August, shows up unannounced, claiming he has a "good gift" for you?

But when I opened the gift, it, for once, was a "good gift." It was a box stacked with old vinyl records. "Are you serious!" I squealed.

Louis smiled. "Mm-hmm! I tested them all, and each one works."

I sifted through the box to see various records from the eighties to the early two thousands. "There're limited edition ones in here! This must've cost a fortune!" I said guiltily.

"No, no," he assured me. "I was helping a buddy of mine's dad clean out his basement. I told him about you, and he let me have those."

In my mind, I thanked the man. I just didn't know why someone would give nearly one hundred records away for free when you could easily make over a thousand dollars.

Louis continued with the gift-giving. He gave my mother new slippers and a cozy robe, while my father got new pots and pans. My father was all ecstatic. "They're nonstick too!" he said.

Louis helped me get the box to my room. "How long are you staying?" I asked him.

He plopped down on my bed and counted up. "Let's see, two-day drive, plus traffic, and that leaves ten days. I'll be here till the fourth."

I smiled. "Wait, so you're gonna be here for New Year's?"

He nodded. "I was even thinking of driving out to Indiana to get some fireworks. You should invite that friend of yours."

Inviting her would be cool. We could even have another sleepover. "I'll ask her if she's free." I pulled out my phone and texted Daisy. She responded almost immediately:

"Yeah, I'm down!"

"We're on," I said.

Louis sat up. "Yes!"

I pushed the box aside and stood up. "Since you're here, do you mind helping out with the café?"

He nodded. "Sure, might as well."

I grinned. "Great! There's a new supply order to fill out. It'll be waiting for you." I walked out of my room as he shouted.

"Hey, wait! You can't do this to me!" I just ignored him and headed back downstairs. Sometimes I wonder why my dad hasn't hired workers yet.

The days seemed to fly by. I guess that's how it always is when you're not in school. All I'd done was write more into my book and sleep. And just as fast as Christmas came, New Year's arrived.

Louis kept his promise and bought some fireworks. Nothing too big, just some sparklers and rockets that shoot into the sky.

Daisy texted me nonstop that morning.

> I'm thinking of resolutions.
> Does getting into your no. 1 college count?
> Speaking of college, you'd better keep talking to me.
> Okay, outfit A or B?
> Do you think saying, "this is gonna be my year" jinxes it?
> I'll say it anyway.
> What time do you want me to come over?
> Please tell me your dad is making a special dessert.

I don't think I'd ever seen anyone as excited for a New Year as she was. She was so excited that she showed up earlier than expected.

"Dinner's not even done yet," I said to her.

Daisy grinned. "Well then, you could show me all those records you got for Christmas." So I led her up to my room. She sat on my bed and seemed almost nervous.

"Here they all are," I said, dragging the box out from my closet. "I haven't had the chance to sort them all yet. I think I'm gonna need a bigger shelf."

I handed Daisy one of the records. "No way, this one is pink!" I showed her the records that had colors like blue and green. There were even records from rock to jazz. "How did you get all these? There are like over a hundred of them," she asked.

I grinned. "Right place, right time?"

Daisy handed the record back to me and threw herself backward on my bed. She sat in silence for a minute before I broke it.

"Are you okay?" I asked.

She paused for a moment. "It's nothing. Um, I just have to tell you something."

Her words seemed to make me uneasy. I thought of all the things it could be. "Well…what is it?" I asked nervously.

Daisy sat up. "I'll tell you later!" She caught herself. "Sorry, I didn't mean to yell like that." It made her nervous, but she still laughed. "I'll tell you later, okay?"

I expected that feeling of uneasiness to go away, but it never did.

Throughout dinner, it was all I could think about. What could she possibly have to say to me?

"Eden, could you pass the bread?" my mother asked from across the table.

"Oh yeah! Sorry." I said, passing the bowl.

She leaned her head on her hand. "What is on your mind now?" She grinned.

I glanced over at Daisy, then back to her, "Oh, uh…fireworks! Yeah! I just can't wait for fireworks." My mother glared over at Louis, who was stuffing his face. "You bought them fireworks!"

His eyes got big, and he started to choke. "Surprise!"

I covered my mouth as she started to grumble. "How many times…ugh…haven't I…"

My father reached over and grabbed her hand. "Marissa, let them have fun. They're young, and it's New Year's Eve!" My mother calmed down before giving us three a look. "Fine. You can have your fireworks, but no missing fingers!" She pointed. We all looked at each other and grinned.

After dinner, Daisy and I watched a horror movie saga until Louis came to get us. He peeked through the doorway with a grin on his face. "Check the time," he whispered.

I pulled out my phone and checked.

"Let me see!" Daisy said, so I turned my phone toward her. "Eleven forty already!" she said, jumping up. Daisy grabbed my hand and pulled me up as well. "C'mon, let's get going!"

We ran downstairs and slipped on our shoes and coats. My mom sat in her chair in the living room next to the lit fireplace. "I'd better not hear of any injuries," she grumbled.

I smiled. "All right!" I loved my mother with my whole heart. She came off as mean sometimes but she just cared a lot.

"There's a park down a few blocks from here. We can go there," Louis said as we left out the door. He led the way as Daisy and I stayed a bit behind him.

"Why doesn't your mother like fireworks?"

I looked at her. "She likes fireworks, but she just thinks they should be left up to the professionals."

Daisy gave me a look, so I explained more. "Apparently, when she was younger, a neighborhood kid got his hands on some illegal fireworks. She said he gathered all the kids on the block to see. Then right as he lit the jumbo firecracker, it malfunctioned."

Daisy's face dropped. "A faulty firework!" She gasped. I grinned and held up my hand. "Yeah! It blew up right in his hand, and he lost three of his fingers!" She looked traumatized. "But who knows! It's just a story after all," I said, trying to lighten up the mood.

It was quiet for most of the walk to the park until Louis finally spoke. "Eden and I used to go to this park all the time."

Daisy lit up. "Really! That's so cool!" She turned and looked at me. "What was your favorite thing to play on?"

I smiled. "Definitely the swings."

"No way! That's mine too! We're going on when we get there."

Louis stopped. "Well then, you're in luck 'cause we're here."

At this particular park, you had to cross a street to get to it. I peeked through the parked cars and looked both ways. "You always wanna look both ways. It may seem like a calm street, but people often speed down it."

Once the coast was clear, we sprinted across to the park. Daisy grinned. "I'll race you to the swings!" I tried sprinting after her, but she was really fast. It was hard to believe we were gonna be seniors next year. Here I was, chasing after a girl who was racing me to the swings at a park; Daisy easily won. I sat on the swing and tried to catch my breath.

"Do you…run track or something?"

She grinned. "I did freshman year and a half of sophomore."

"Why did you stop?" I asked.

She laughed. "Right before the biggest race of the season, I had a bad fall at a practice."

I gave her a sympathetic expression. "Then what?"

Daisy sighed. "I was put off the team and temporarily suspended from any ankle-stressing activities. That meant running, roller skating, ice skating, exercising, and so on."

I sighed as I gave myself a push on the swing. "I feel so bad. That must've crushed you."

She gave a sad, soft smile. "It did, but time heals all wounds. Plus, I met you. You may not realize it, but you've done so much for me."

I smiled. "You've done so much for me as well. I feel as if you've done more for me than I have for you."

Daisy started laughing. "Just you simply talking to me is enough." She paused. "About what I was gonna tell you—"

Louis then waved over to us. "It's time!"

I hopped off the swing. "Race you!" I grinned.

"No fair!" she said, chasing after me. We then all gathered around and started counting.

"Ten…!" Daisy smiled at me.

"Nine…!" I smiled at her.

"Eight…seven…!" Her smile turned into a subtle grin.

"Six…five…!"

"Four…three…!" Louis got ready to light the firework.

"Two…one…!" Daisy grabbed my hands.

"Happy New Year!" we all shouted.

Louis lit the firework, and it shot up into the sky, but it wasn't the only one. I guess people all had the same idea. I looked down at Daisy. She bit her lip and said something, but I couldn't hear over the screech and booms of the fireworks.

"What did you say?" I shouted.

She looked embarrassed. "Nothing! Never mind!"

Louis tossed us a box of sparklers. "I got these for you guys."

Daisy smiled. "I love these!"

I grabbed a lighter, and we put two sparklers together before lighting them.

Daisy smiled and said, "Thank you for these past few months. It really made my year."

Louis ran over with a strip of small firecrackers. "Wanna light one, Daisy?"

She looked at him with her eyes all wide. "No! No, I'm good. I would like to keep my fingers!" Louis and I started laughing. "It's not funny!" she said before lightly pushing me.

I wiped the tear from my eye. "What were you trying to say earlier?"

Daisy, too embarrassed now, just stood there quietly before getting another sparkler out of the box. "Let's just finish up the fireworks," she said.

We laughed the whole way back from the park.

"We should make this a tradition," Daisy said.

Louis agreed with her. "Yeah, E'ed! It would be such a good idea."

I smiled at them as we went into the house. "That would be fun."

I looked into the living room before going upstairs; my mother wasn't there. I assumed she went to bed, so I went back to my room.

Daisy had thrown herself onto my bed.

"Hey, uh, I'm sorry you have to sleep next to me again. I promise I'm working on getting an air mattress," I said, but she just started laughing.

"I don't mind. Plus your bed is mad comfy." I smiled at her before getting extra covers from the closet.

She seemed different, like something was bothering her. "Is everything okay?" I asked. She just gave her usual smile and downplayed it.

I stopped prying. I figured it was a matter that she was uncomfortable discussing with me, so I lay down. She didn't speak. Was it something I did? I peeked over, but she was asleep. I sighed and closed my eyes. It wasn't long until I fell asleep as well.

"Wake up! Wake up!"

I jolted up to see Daisy in a panic. "W-What's going on?" I asked in a delirious tone of voice.

"T-There was crashing coming from downstairs!" I paused and looked toward the door.

Then suddenly, there was a loud *thud*. I hopped out of bed, "Could someone have broken in?" I asked myself. The idea didn't leave my mind as I grabbed a bat from my closet. It was New Year's, and people could do crazy things.

Daisy, scared, followed behind me as I crept down the hallway. I started heading down the stairs when she grabbed me. "Stop! What if they're armed?" she whispered.

I took a deep breath and put my hands on her shoulders. "If anything happens, you go and wake up Louis and my father." Tears started filling up my eyes. "I have to go check. My mother is down there. I love her too much to let anything happen to her."

Daisy didn't speak, but she gave me a look, saying, "Go do what you must."

I turned and crept down the stairs. I tried blinking my eyes in the engulfing darkness, hoping that I could see something. I reached my hand over to the light switch while still gripping the bat tightly in my other.

When I turned the light on, I let out the loudest scream I ever had in my life. Daisy came running down the stairs. When she saw the scene, she let out a gasp and covered her mouth.

"M-Mom?" I muttered as tears filled up my eyes. On the floor was my mother.

My father and Louis came sprinting down the stairs. "Marissa!" my father called out as he rushed over to her side.

I couldn't do anything. I just stood still. "Call an ambulance!" Louis shouted at me as he ran to check for intruders.

I just couldn't move. *Move. Move. Move!* I shouted in my mind. It felt like the floor had been pulled from under me.

Daisy shook me. "Eden! I'm calling an ambulance right now!"

There was blood, a lot of blood. "Marissa, stay with me!" my father cried out. In the distance, a siren could be heard.

Everything seemed to go in slow motion—the paramedics coming, Louis telling me to get in the car with him and Daisy, and waiting for hours. Daisy held my hand in the waiting room. She was quiet and completely out of it.

A doctor finally came in. "Mr. Aubert?" she called out. My father stood up and met up with the doctor. "About Marissa," the doctor started, "her osteosarcoma had come back even stronger." My father gasped. "I'm assuming she didn't inform you, Mr. Aubert."

My father stood still. "What else?" he asked.

The doctor sighed. "She had a visit with Dr. Kim a few weeks ago. She was approached with the option of chemotherapy again, but she refused."

Tears began filling up my father's eyes. "Is she going to be okay?"

The doctor paused for a moment, then spoke the words nobody would ever want to hear. "She took a fall and suffered extreme head trauma. She has an extensive brain bleed, and we're afraid that she won't make it through the night. I suggest you and your family say your final goodbyes."

My father fell to the floor and cried, "No! This can't be! This is all a dream!" He looked over and grabbed Louis by the collar and shook him. "Tell me this is all a dream!" But Louis just stood silently and cried softly. My father finally stopped shaking him and released his shirt.

"No, this is reality, Dad," he whispered.

I sat watching as Louis held up my father. Daisy let go of my hand and put it on my shoulder. "Go, go join them. You don't wanna regret it."

I wiped the tears from my eyes and stood up before joining them.

The doctor led us through the dim, quiet halls to her room. It was quiet with the occasional beeping of the machines. My father rushed to her side and cried, "Don't leave me, *mon amour.*"

Louis sat down by her side and held her hand. "Mama! Please stay strong."

They talked to her for hours, but I just sat in the corner of the room. I was still in shock. I couldn't comprehend what had happened. I finally took a deep breath and walked over to her. My father and Louis had fallen asleep by her side. "Mama, I—"

I was cut off by the beeping of her machines speeding up. "What did I do!" I shouted.

My father and Louis woke up. "Get a doctor!" Louis shouted at me. I was able to move this time. I ran out into the hall to see a nurse passing by. "Help me! It's my mother!" The nurse heard the beeping and sprinted down the hall.

"Code blue: room 114 B. Code blue: all on floor staff report" echoed over the speakers. Within seconds, a group of doctors and nurses came sprinting down the hall.

"Clear out!" one shouted.

"What's going on?" I asked. "What's happening?"

A nurse grabbed me. "Honey, your mother is in cardiac arrest. I need you to wait out here."

I slumped down to the floor. "No, no, no, no," I mumbled over and over, and I covered my ears. The air seemed so thin and hard to suck in. I choked on air and drowned in my words.

A nurse knelt next to me and said, "Just breathe, sweetheart."

But no matter how hard I tried, it didn't work. I looked over to see my father. He sat on the floor with his hands over his head; Louis had been trying to calm him down.

After a few minutes, a doctor came out of the room taking his gloves off. "I'm afraid she's gone." My father cried out even louder. I had never seen him cry like that. "We'll get the release forms ready."

I fell on my hands and knees. "No! She can't be gone! She was just fine! We just had dinner with her! I was just talking to her!"

The nurse rubbed my back. "It happens like that sometimes, honey."

By the time we left, the sun was already up. I felt so empty, like I forgot something important to me.

We all got into the car, and the whole way home was quiet. We walked through the door into the empty house. I peered into the living room toward her chair. "How could I not notice?" I asked myself. I slowly walked upstairs and threw myself onto my bed, and I just cried. I cried for hours, maybe days? I don't know. After a while, you just lose a sense of time.

VIII

Words and Regrets

Seasons change, and life moves on; but for those stuck in the past, time stays still.

For the duration of the funeral, I was motionless. I didn't mutter a word the whole time. After it was over, Louis went back down to college. My father started working in the café again and seemed better overall.

As for me, I was the one stuck. I didn't leave my room, I didn't open the curtains, I didn't answer texts, I didn't go to school, and I barely ate. All I did was sit in my room, mindlessly scrolling through social media. How long had it been? I checked the date, and it was March 10. *Oh?* I thought to myself for a second. *Guess it's been a few months.*

Over that time, Daisy had been stopping by. She brought the schoolwork I missed, but I didn't do it; the work just piled up in my room along with all the clothes on my floor. Why am I like this?

I finally put my phone down. The sun was starting to set. I heard footsteps in the hall, then my father knocked on the door. "*Ma fille*," he called out to me. It had been a while since he called me that. "Daisy is here. She wants to talk to you."

I put my hand over my face and yelled, "Tell her to go home!" My father let out a sad breath. "Eden," he paused. "Just hear her out."

I took a moment to look around my room. It was cluttered with clothes and cans. I took a deep breath. "Fine." I stood up and slipped on my shoes.

Before leaving, I caught a glimpse of myself in a mirror. My face was thin and pale, my hair was grown out in the back, and eyebags polluted my face; I looked sick.

I walked downstairs to see that everything had changed. There was a new cloth on the dining table, the living room was painted a new color, and more pictures hung on the wall. It felt all so new, like an impostor.

I stopped and looked over at Daisy. She had been sitting at the kitchen island before she stood up. I could tell that she wanted to say something about my appearance; instead, she just kept quiet and looked away.

"Let's go," she said before heading toward the door.

"We could just talk here," I said, but she turned around.

"No, you need to go out." I just rolled my eyes and followed her.

We walked down the sidewalk in silence for a while.

"I've been helping out at the café in your place."

I sighed. "Look, we don't need your pity or help."

Daisy turned toward me. "Well, your father actually asked me to."

I laughed sarcastically. "So now you're here to replace me? Of course, because you're so perfect! He always liked you better anyways."

She gasped. "Eden, no! That's not what I'm trying to do! Nor should you say that!"

I rolled my eyes at her. "Please!"

Daisy sighed. "We're here." I looked up to see the park, the one we were at on New Year's. We crossed the street, and she had me sit down on a bench next to her.

"So what the hell are you gonna talk to me about?"

Daisy looked down to the floor. "You need to come back to school."

I scoffed in her face. "That's all you dragged me here for?" I stood up. "Screw this."

She yelled after me. "They're gonna revoke your scholarships and kick you out!"

I turned toward her again in a fit of rage. "Does it look like I care?"

Daisy stood up. "You should!"

I clenched my jaw. "Well, I'm sorry I'm not perfect like you!" She tried to talk, but I just kept going on. "I'm sorry I'm not rich! I'm sorry I don't have a new car; I don't even have a mother anymore!"

She tried to speak again. "Eden, listen!"

My words kept going, and they only sharpened. "No! Just shut the hell up! Your kindness is pitiful and is like an insult to me! You will never know what it's like to be in my position!"

Daisy began to hold back tears at this point. She took the clip out of her hair; it was a daisy. "Give this back to me when you come back to your senses."

I just threw the clip on the floor. "No! I wish I never met you that day! Cause maybe those friends of yours were right! Are you really nice, or do you just think I'm stupid!"

She began to cry. "You don't mean that, do you?"

I clenched my fist. "I mean every bit! You think you're better than everyone like an entitled little bitch! You think you know me, but you'll never understand!"

Daisy gave me a cold gaze, unlike any I had ever seen. "I do understand! I lost my dad when I was nine! Nine, Eden! I was a child! I know what it's like to not have money! Okay, and for the record, I never wanted any of this crap! I could care less about money! I thought you were different, but you're just like everyone else."

I released my fist. "Just go away and never come back."

Daisy sighed. "You would like that, wouldn't you? Maybe I won't come back." With that, she turned around, and my heart sank. What have I done?

She began heading out of the park as she cried.

"Daisy, wait!" I screamed, but it was too late.

At the same time, Daisy was crossing the street, a man, who had been fired from his job mere hours before, came speeding drunk down the street. It's crazy how things happen so fast. How fast a life can change and how someone's life can get taken from them.

My heart seemed to plummet, and I felt tears welling in my eyes. I felt a shaking in my chest like shock washing over my body. My hands shook, and I couldn't even mutter a word. My legs were stuck in their place. It happened again, and I couldn't even move an inch.

Daisy had been hit, and it was all my fault. I fell to the ground. What else could I do? I was weak.

"Call an ambulance!" people screamed as they swarmed around her body on the road. A woman, who saw everything, rushed over to me, "Ah! Are you okay? Was she your friend? Oh my! You're Eden, I'll call your father!"

I couldn't respond. All I could mumble was "I killed her." I said it over and over until my father pulled me off the pavement. "Eden! It's going to be all right! Let's meet them at the hospital."

I grabbed her clip off the ground. "I have to give it back to her!"

He pulled me into a hug, and I just cried. "It's all my fault! I killed Daisy! It should've been me!"

My father brushed the hair off my face. "*Ma fille*, be strong. Now we must go if we're going to meet them there." I sat in the passenger seat, and we headed off toward the hospital.

Throughout the whole car ride, he tried to get in contact with Daisy's mother. It was no use, however. We got out of the car and were immediately shuffled into the waiting room.

Upon seeing those beige walls and blue chairs, I felt sick. *Why am I here again?* I thought. I sat down while covering my mouth. There I was again, waiting for hours in a sad-smelling room.

It was around ten at night when Daisy's mother arrived. She looked around the room until she saw my father. "Mrs. Harrow-Hamilton," he said standing up.

She smiled. "Please just call me Mary." She swallowed. "Thank you for staying here. I tried to get here as soon as I could. New York is farther than I thought."

She turned toward me. "You must be Eden."

I looked at her, and I just started crying, "It's all my fault! It's all my fault! I killed her!"

But Mrs. Harrow didn't get mad or even yell at me; instead, she hugged me carefully.

"It's not your fault, sweetheart. It's nobody's, not even the driver. He didn't know he would hit someone today. You've gone through a lot. Don't be so hard on yourself." Even though her words were sweet, guilt still filled inside of me like water in my lungs.

After another hour, the doctor came and told us we could see her. When I walked into the room, I nearly lost my breath. She lay in the hospital bed hooked up to numerous machines.

"What have I done?"

The doctor looked at his clipboard and said, "She's in a medically induced coma at the moment. Her injuries are extensive, and to be honest, we are not sure how she survived an impact of its speed."

I turned, nearly in tears again. "Will she live?"

The doctor paused. "Her pulse is severely weak. I'm afraid she won't have long. If she does somehow pull through, her life won't be the same."

I sat down on the stool next to Daisy's bed. "I'm so sorry," I whispered.

Her mother put her coat back on. "I'll go get some stuff to spend the night. You can spend some alone time with her in the meantime." She turned, and my father followed her out the door.

I turned back toward Daisy. Her face and arms were all scraped up, and bruises filled her body. I traced my finger down her scraped arm until I got to her finger. I looked down to see a familiar golden ring with a beautiful green gem; it was the ring I gave her.

I just lost it. "I'm so sorry! I should've never said those things! I didn't mean it! This is all my fault! Forgive me, Daisy!" I cried over and over.

When I looked back up with my watery eyes, I saw a single tear fall from her eye. It was as if she heard me. "Could you ever forgive me?" I asked her as if she would respond to me. I gently grabbed her hand. "I will never forgive myself." I swore.

I leaned my head on the bedside. My heart ached extensively. "I had figured it out, Daisy." I closed my eyes. "The answer is that I've liked you all along," I whispered.

"Eden, sweetheart. Please wake up." I opened my eyes to see Mrs. Harrow. "Please go home and get some sleep," she said to me. So I grabbed my jacket and stood up. I glanced back at Daisy one last time before leaving.

A few days later, I was getting a bouquet of daisies for her when I got a call.

Daisy passed away on March fifteenth at twelve o five in the afternoon. I fell to my knees and cried. What else could I do?

So I sat alone in my room. I finally closed the photo album. Her services were probably over by now. I still felt a massive amount of guilt. Maybe, just maybe, if I hadn't said those things, Daisy would still be alive. So I killed Daisy Harrow; it was all because of me.

IX

To You a Year Later

One year had passed since Daisy's death. I'd been doing a lot better since then. I'd been talking to a therapist, and with help, I decided to finally visit Daisy's grave. Dr. Shultz said to me, "Don't go if you feel as if you're not ready." But I thought I finally was. I owed her my life.

With time, I learned how to forgive myself, though guilt never goes away. So I sucked up my fears and walked down to the cemetery. In one hand was a bouquet for my mother, and in my other was a fruit tart.

I first walked over to my mother's grave; I knelt and replaced the old flowers with new ones. "Hi, Mom, I know it's been a minute since we last talked," I started. "Louis finally settled down and got a girlfriend of his own in California. As for Dad, he's planning on opening a new restaurant." I smiled. "He said that he'll give me the café when I graduate college."

I paused. "Right! About college, I'm gonna graduate high school in a few weeks. I ended up getting into my dream college, just as you said I would." I sighed and smiled. "We all miss you."

I brushed my finger across the lettering on her stone before standing up. "I just know you're in a better place now. A place where no sickness can hold you back."

I began walking toward Daisy's grave. My father had given me the location some time ago, just in case I wanted to go.

As I got closer, I got more nervous. What would I say? How would I even start?

I peeked around the corner to see Mrs. Harrow sitting by Daisy's grave. I instinctively hid behind a close by tree hoping that she didn't see me. "It's okay, Eden, you can come out," she said to me. It felt like déjà vu; this happened before.

I stepped from behind the tree with an awkward smile. "Hello! I'm sorry, I didn't know you would be here! I can come back another day!" Mrs. Harrow just smiled and gestured for me to sit with her on the picnic blanket.

I gingerly walked over and sat down across from her. I looked down and unboxed the fruit tart and placed it next to Daisy's flowers. "She was always a fan of your baking, wasn't she?"

I smiled. "Yeah. But she liked my dad's more."

Mrs. Harrow began laughing. "I don't think that's true!"

I gave a confused look. "What?"

Her laugh turned into a smile. "Oh, how she would talk about you. Now, I wasn't home very often, but when I was, you were all she'd talk about."

I was shocked. "Really?"

She nodded. "*She loved you* more than you could ever know."

I looked down. "But I…killed her…"

Mrs. Harrow placed her hand upon my shoulder. "It wasn't your fault. Even if it was, do you think Daisy would hate you?"

She was right. Daisy just wasn't that kind of person. She pointed at my chest. "You can only find peace if you truly *forgive yourself*, in there."

I smiled. "Thank you. That's just what I needed to hear."

She smiled. "Would you like to come by my place for tea? I have some things to give to you." I nodded, and we went off.

I sat in the passenger side of Mrs. Harrow's luxury car. I felt a bit nervous. I'd never ridden in a car this fancy. I guess she noticed because she smiled over at me. "Don't be nervous. I can tell you some stories about Daisy on the way if you would like." I nodded, and we set off.

She told me stories about her, like when she was seven, she climbed up a tree just so she could read her books for longer. It was nice hearing about a Daisy I didn't know.

After some driving, we finally arrived. I looked out the window to see a huge, high-rise condo building. I knew Daisy was rich, just not this rich. We rode the elevator to the thirtieth floor where we got out. "Don't mind the mess, we're in the middle of moving," she said, turning the key in the door.

"And here we are!" she said, revealing a huge, bare condo. My eyes immediately looked at the huge window that displayed the city. I was kinda jealous that she got to see this view every day. Yet I couldn't imagine how lonely it was for her.

"Come sit. I just put the tea on the stove," Mrs. Harrow said, directing me toward the table.

I walked over and sat down on the fabric chair across from her. "I just want to thank you."

I looked up. "For what?" I asked.

She scrunched up her lips and looked back to me. "James, Daisy's father, died of a heart attack on her ninth birthday. It absolutely destroyed her, but she was strong. I don't know how she did it."

I looked down. "I'm so sorry. I never knew."

Mrs. Harrow nodded. "She's not one to share a whole lot about herself."

I nodded in return. "So what happened next?" I asked, but she paused for a moment before beginning.

"I selfishly threw myself deeper into work because in my mind I was giving her a better life." She sighed. "I uprooted her, moved her downtown, and I was never home." I could hear the hurt in her voice, though she tried not to let it show. "I just wish I could turn back time and just spend more of it with her."

I gave a sad smile. "We two are alike."

She smiled as the kettle whistled. "Give me a moment," she said while heading toward the stove. "Is lemon okay?" I nodded back to her, and she brought over the teacups. "You can have your tea. I'm going to grab the things." I took a sip of the tea as she left. It felt nice seeing where Daisy lived for all those years, but just not as nice under the circumstances.

"Okay, here we are!" Mrs. Harrow said, carrying a large box filled with things. "I left her room untouched for the longest time, but I finally had to go through it recently. Oh, but these are the things that I couldn't bear to get rid of or donate." She put the box on the table. "Please take anything you would like."

I stood up and looked at the contents of the box. There were things like hair clips, her favorite books, and jewelry. I reached for a smaller yellow box.

"Oh, those! Daisy wrote letters every day. I didn't touch them, because they were all addressed to you."

I smiled and pulled out one. I read "Dear Eden," and my heart sank. "I'll take them to read later." I carefully placed the box aside and continued looking.

I grabbed a few items to keep, but as I looked again, I saw something sparkle from the bottom of the box. I reached in and pulled out a gold ring with a green gem. It was once again the one I had gotten her. I was fighting tears at this point; I guess it finally hit me.

"Oh, that ring. She told me that it was her favorite piece of jewelry." She paused for a moment. "Let me get something." As she left, I just started to cry. Daisy's actually gone. I quickly wiped my tears as she came back.

In her hand was an empty necklace chain. I handed her the ring, and she slipped it through the chain. "Now she will always be with you!" I smiled and just started crying. Mrs. Harrow hugged me. "You're a good person, Eden."

I walked down the sidewalk toward the train station. The cold spring wind blew my shoulder-length hair. I reached into my pocket and felt something familiar. I pulled out a daisy-shaped hair clip and just started laughing. "Of course." I played with it in my hand and gave a sideways smile. "I guess we never got to see the field of flowers together." I gave a soft smile as I looked up to the sky. "Just wait for me, okay? So then we can."

X

To You in Ten Years

"Eden! We're about to start!"

A woman with long black hair stood up and shut her computer. "RJ, you can wait two seconds! I just finished writing *Field of Flowers*."

RJ walked into the room looking visually stressed. "I'm glad, but the line is through the door, Eden!"

Eden paused. "Really?"

He gave a disappointed expression. "Like you're not a *New York Times* number one best-selling author and wrote seven successful books so far."

Eden smiled. "Okay, okay, I get it."

She walked through the door and into the lobby of the café. "Thank you, everyone, for coming today!" The crowd of people cheered. "This café belonged to my father long before it was mine. But we are here today to celebrate the renaming of it."

The crowd roared even louder. "The new name is dedicated to an old friend of mine, Daisy.

She was tragically killed after becoming a victim of a drunk driver." She took a deep breath. "So I would like to welcome you to *Daisy's Place!*" Eden sat down as everyone cheered. "Now let's start the book signing!"

People of many different ages came to see her that day. She was happy to see so many people who enjoyed her work. RJ slumped down next to her. "Man! That was a lot!"

Eden smiled. "It was nice, though."

He stood up. "I'm gonna clean the back."

Eden nodded and started putting her stuff away as a young girl came into the shop. She had long blonde hair and beautiful green eyes. "Oh, sweetheart! The book signing just ended."

The young girl just smiled. "Could you possibly point me toward the fantasy section?"

Eden smiled and pointed. "It's right over there." The girl ran off into the aisles and came back with a particular book. It was blue and had a Ferris wheel of flowers on the cover. The girl handed the book to Eden.

She smiled at the girl. "You read *Carnival of Flowers*?"

The girl smiled back. "It's only the best series ever! No offense to you." The girl laughed.

Eden handed the book back to her. "Here, you can have it for free. Just promise you'll come back, and we can talk all about it."

The girl smiled. "Thank you so much!"

All of a sudden, a frantic woman ran through the café doors. "Lilly! There you are!" The woman apologized. "I am so sorry! She tends to wander off."

Eden just smiled. "It's okay!"

The woman looked at her daughter. "Let's go now."

The girl looked back and smiled familiarly as she walked out with her mother.

The café sat silent and empty. Eden smiled to herself. "It's nice to see you too, Daisy."

End

Dear Eden,

Well, if you're reading this, that means I'm on a confidence boost or something happened to me. I'm not too confident often, so I fear that it will most likely be the latter.

You'll probably find some way to blame yourself because that's just who you are. And if you *are*, know that it's not your fault, and you know that I could never be mad at you.

I actually wanna come clean about a few things…

I may have lied a few times. To start, our meeting wasn't a coincidence at all. I knew for a long time that you worked there. I just never had enough confidence to go up and talk to you. I felt like we lived in completely different worlds, and I feared that you would hate me or see me like some basic popular girl. I actually had known about you for a long time.

The first time we *really* met was on a rainy day in freshman year. It was downpouring so hard that day, and I stood by the door hoping it would stop! That's when you offered me your umbrella. That's the moment I started liking you. However, I think that was just a normal Tuesday for you.

After that, I found out that the other students beat down on you a lot. I figured that you'd lump me with everyone else. So while they wrote harmful things on your locker, I would stay after school and paint over it.

The soup incident was one of my favorites! It was absolutely hilarious seeing Rose get so angry. Though I never heard the end of it.

I was even in a lot of your classes, but even then, I was too cowardly to talk to you.

But that day when you knocked over the book cart, I was in the next aisle. I felt that it was the stars giving me a chance, so I leapt.

My second lie was me coming back to get *Carnival of Flowers*. It was never on your cart in the first place! It was just my sorry excuse to come and talk to you.

So there! You've been fooled by the one and only "Goddess of Lincoln Academy," Daisy Harrow. Hahaha! I don't regret a thing if you ask me. If I were to go back in time, I would do the same thing. No, I would talk to you sooner. So I do have one regret, and it's that.

Yours truly,
Daisy Harrow

Dear Eden,

Oh! We've been hanging out for a few days now. I absolutely crushed you in Smash today! I think that I should go easier on you. It would give me the opportunity to request a rematch. In the end, more matches!

My friends have been asking where I've been. I've just been telling them "Doing more important things," and hey! I wouldn't be lying.

Yours truly,
Daisy Harrow

Dear Eden,

Gosh! I stayed up so late last night because hey, summer isn't over until you fall asleep on the final night! I was scrambling around in the morning. You didn't text me, though! I figured that you were also running behind.

Ugh! Joey and all those kids just need to leave you alone! They're getting on my last nerves!

PS: You kinda seem like you're ignoring me today. You literally swerved and pulled a 180 and went to the bathroom. I fear that I did something wrong, and it really scares me. I'll ask you in second period.

Yours truly,
Daisy Harrow

Dear Eden,

    Thank you for everything you did for me that day. Like standing up to my (ex) friends. I just wish that I was better at being that cool.
    But that wish that I made on the roof, I'll tell you now…
    My wish was that you overcome your past and make lots of friends and become super successful. I have a strong feeling that the stars will grant my wish, as they did once before. And what was that wish? That you'd be my friend.

Yours truly,
Daisy Harrow

A Word from the Author

Hello! My name is Kaylee Davenport. I am the author of this book. I would like to start by thanking you for reading *Field of Flowers*. This book is a big part of me. Honestly, it just started as something I was writing during my free time in school. And look at it now!

 This book is actually a rewrite of an earlier and shorter version I had written. I had written the original idea when I was in eighth grade, and I started and finished this version in my freshman year of high school. Between the two, there are a few differences, but they ultimately follow the same plot idea.

 If you were to tell the past me, that girl who sat on her computer night after night working on *FoF*, that you were holding the book right now, she would laugh. Because she believed that she couldn't possibly publish it, or even finish it for that matter. But I had people who stood by me and cheered me on. Whether it was my mother who listened to my crazed ideas, my dad who helped me publish it, or my friends who cheered on for another chapter to read.

 So to you dear reader: Never stop chasing your dreams because if you keep running, you're bound to catch them, no matter how far they seem.

About the Author

Kaylee Davenport has always loved writing ever since she was little. She loved writing because she got to see people's reactions to what she wrote. She often writes during her spare time and shows her ideas to her friends. She grew up in Chicago, so she has always been inspired by all the art and creativity throughout the city. It was her driving force to create this book, the book that was written through the quiet time she spent alone in second-period study during her freshman year of high school. She feels that there is nothing left but improvement from here for her.

Printed in the USA
CPSIA information can be obtained
at www.ICGtesting.com
LVHW011042210924
791651LV00013B/597